THE

Velvet

Hammer

BOOKS BY FAITH BALDWIN

Three Women
Departing Wings
Alimony
The Office-Wife
The Incredible Year
Make-believe
Today's Virtue
Skyscraper
Week-end Marriage
District Nurse
Self-made Woman
Beauty
White-collar Girl
Love's a Puzzle
Innocent Bystander
Wife Versus Secretary
Within a Year
Honor Bound
American Family
The Puritan Strain
The Moon's Our Home
Private Duty
The Girls of Divine Corners
Men Are Such Fools!
That Man Is Mine
The Heart Has Wings
Twenty-four Hours a Day
Manhattan Nights
Enchanted Oasis
Rich Girl, Poor Girl
Hotel Hostess
The High Road
Career By Proxy
White Magic
Station Wagon Set
Rehearsal for Love
"Something Special"
Letty and the Law
Medical Center

And New Stars Burn
Temporary Address: Reno
The Heart Remembers
Blue Horizons
Breath of Life
Five Women in Three Novels
The Rest of My Life With You
Washington, U.S.A.
You Can't Escape
He Married a Doctor
Change of Heart
Arizona Star
A Job for Jenny
No Private Heaven
Woman on Her Way
Sleeping Beauty
Give Love the Air
Marry for Money
They Who Love
The Golden Shoestring
Look Out for Liza
The Whole Armor
The Juniper Tree
Face Toward the Spring
Three Faces of Love
Many Windows
Blaze of Sunlight
Testament of Trust
The West Wind
Harvest of Hope
The Lonely Man
Living By Faith
There Is a Season
Evening Star
The Velvet Hammer

POETRY

Sign Posts
Widow's Walk

Faith Baldwin

THE

Velvet

Hammer

HOLT, RINEHART AND WINSTON

New York · Chicago · San Francisco

SBN:03–076385–1.

Designer: Marge Flock

Published, March, 1969

Second Printing, April, 1969

With love, to Christine Pennock with whom for many years I have shared many memories, one of them of a young woman who looked (so the gentleman caller said) like a ruined castle.

THE
Velvet
Hammer

One

<hr>

I T REQUIRED about twenty minutes to drive from the hospital to the Brand house, longer if the traffic was heavy. Meg Brand's shift ended theoretically at four, but she rarely was able to leave promptly. Mrs. Elgin, Meg's efficient, demanding, and sometimes exasperating superior, often summoned her to after-hours conferences. The hospital, like most hospitals, was very busy and frequently understaffed. It was not a big university-connected institution such as the one, in another state, in which Meg had trained, but it was large enough to serve the town of Melton and neighboring communities. It had a fine nursing school of which Mrs. Elgin was supervisor, a good staff, very modern equipment, and it was very well run. Of the school, Mrs. Elgin—whose late husband had been in the Navy—often remarked that she ran a taut ship.

Meg, since her promotion following the breakdown of Mrs. Elgin's previous assistant, had found, not to her astonishment, that her responsibility for inevitable paper work had greatly increased. As any good officer must, Mrs. Elgin firmly believed in delegating responsibility.

During the years—how long is forever?—that Meg had worked at the hospital, she had found it difficult to explain to her mother-in-law, Cornelia Brand, why she was so frequently late. Mrs. Brand was under the impression, probably gained by observation of the workmen she employed, that an eight-hour day consisted of eight hours.

Naturally Cornelia was on the Hospital Board. Years ago, her money, mainly inherited from her parents, had founded the Brand Memorial in Melton, a town which had itself been founded by her father's ancestors. There had been a small hospital in Melton, but people in need of intricate surgery or with something more grave than the run-of-the-mill diseases had been obliged to take a long trip by car, train, or ambulance to the nearest big city. After the death of her husband, Andrew Brand, early in the Second World War, Cornelia had conceived the project of transforming the inadequate facilities into a good, accredited institution. It had taken a great deal of money, other people's as well as her own, but she was an expert fund raiser. It had also taken time, more than two decades, to produce the hospital in which her daughter-in-law now labored—and, in which, almost three years ago she had labored in another sense and there been delivered of Andrew Brand, the Third.

During those more than twenty years, old doctors had died or retired; one or two had moved away, but others had come. There were a number of them now, from Melton and the nearby towns, well trained and hard working, and their patients need not go elsewhere for treatment or repairs.

When the new hospital had risen from the metaphorical ashes of the old, Mrs. Brand (her well-shod foot on a shovel as she cast the first clod) had named it the Melton Brand Memorial in honor of her parents and her husband, but it had long since been shortened to Brand. The Brand house (originally built and added to by the Meltons) was the town show place. Big, ugly, domineering, but extremely comfortable, the original structure had been built in the eighties, complete with manicured lawns, fine gardens, huge old trees, clipped shrubbery and even a maze, Mr. Melton having traveled in England. The iron stags no longer stood at bay, although, as the craze for the Victorian grew, Cornelia now and then threatened to bring them back from storage. Some

2

chipped-nosed statues and a fountain or two had been banished. The porte-cochère was intact, and the carriage house was now a garage. All the buildings were of stone, except the conservatory, and Cornelia had not sold one acre of meadowland, orchard, or woods, although land prices were rising. She had no wish to halt Melton's progress—indeed, she encouraged it—but she did not fancy split-level houses or Cape Cod cottages creeping up to her back door.

In Melton there was Brand Avenue (residential), Brand Lane (which did lead to split-levels), and also a welter. of Brand and Melton enterprises, including the Melton factory.

Cornelia Brand contributed generously to all the local places of worship, but the stained-glass windows in memory of her parents and her husband had been installed in her own church and now as a memorial to her son, she was contemplating enlarged recreational facilities, or perhaps a small chapel. She had long conferences about this with the comparatively new minister. The Reverend Mr. Jones, before he accepted his present position, had been briefed on the wisdom of listening to Mrs. Brand on all matters, particularly those concerning his parish. He had succeeded a man named Byrne, who had resigned. At that time an irreverent remark had gone the rounds, ascribed to Dr. Scott, Chief of Staff at the hospital. "Well," the good gray doctor had presumably said, "there's one Byrne snatched from the Brand!"

This comment had, in due time, reached Cornelia, who smiled and dismissed it. She didn't like Dr. Scott any better than he liked her. None of her friends knew why. He had once been her personal physician, though not for a number of years. But no amount of maneuvering on her part could budge him from his position at the hospital. He was too well liked by others on the Board and by a great many people in the town and outside of it.

As Meg drove to the Brand house—she never thought of it as home, although she'd lived there before Andrew was

3

born, and ever since—she was thinking not of Dr. Scott, Chief of Staff, but of his son, Charles.

Presently she turned off the main road, took a blacktop which narrowed down and then widened into a turnoff, labeled "Scenic Rest" by the Garden Club. There was plenty of parking space, a high protective stone railing, and a wide view of rolling hills, ridges, and small valleys. It was a popular place for lovers; the Garden Club had tried to put a stop to that, but short of hiring an all-night watchman they could not; the most they could do was to persuade a prowl car to drive up on regular patrol. It was also a good place for people to stop and refresh themselves with natural beauty—the Club had voted against a small picnic ground—and a good place in which to relax and permit any recent annoyance to blow away on the wind. Meg often stopped here when she had had a particularly tiring day, or simply in order to think— to try to understand the past, evaluate the present, and speculate upon the future—before returning to the Brand house. Cornelia, unless detained at one of her numerous board or committee meetings, was always home shortly after four to indulge in a little playtime with her grandson. She would have tea—iced in summer, hot in winter—and receive friends who, knowing her habits might drop in for tea, advice, money, gossip, or an admixture of these.

Thinking now of Charles Scott, who had returned to Melton to enter into practice with his father, Meg smiled. She had smiled this morning at something he'd said when she encountered him in a corridor and he had remarked, "You should do that more often."

"Do what, Dr. Scott?"

"Scotty to you," he had said. "Smile. It's becoming to you and, for me, pleasantly disturbing."

She had smiled again; gambits such as this had been familiar to her ever since she had entered training.

Charles Scott had been born in Melton, and from there

had gone away to school and the university. He'd served his internship in a big city hospital before going into the Navy. He'd been back home since early spring, somewhat against his liking, or so the rumor ran, for he'd wanted a city practice and then specialization. But his father had had a heart attack.

By now, Meg reflected, Charles Scott knew as much or more about her—that she was the widow of Cornelia Brand's only son who had been killed in Saigon when a bomb had exploded outside of a restaurant-bar. Also that she had met Andy, a correspondent for a wire service, in England, where he'd been between assignments and she had been visiting her aunt shortly after taking her M.A.

Probably Charles Scott also knew that she and Andy had been in Greece on their wedding trip when the Saigon assignment came through, and it was certain that he'd heard Cornelia had not been at the wedding; she'd been on a world cruise and had not been notified in time to jump ship and fly to London.

After a while Meg backed her car, turned and headed for Cornelia's where it was not as easy to think, even when alone in what had been Andy's room, kept by his mother much as it had been in his prep-school days.

It is hard to think in a shrine. One can, of course, contemplate and meditate, but to think—especially about one's self—is sacrilege. The whole house was, in effect, a shrine for Andrew Brand, the Third. It would be in this house that small Andrew would grow up. From here he would go to his father's and grandfather's school, and on to their university. Unless I can prevent it, Meg thought, driving toward teatime.

Possibly, before that, Cornelia would be gathered to her illustrious Melton ancestors who had been routinely educated and whose talents were chiefly for making money. The Brands, however, had been honed to a fine cutting edge by education and what is known as position.

However, Cornelia was only in her late fifties and seemingly in excellent health.

Meg told herself, as she did at least twice a day: "We have to get away." But how?

She and Andy, before their marriage, had discussed the possibility of her pregnancy, and she'd said, "I'd like to have a baby."

"So would I—I have ideas about how to bring up a kid and how not to—but it wouldn't be sensible. God knows where they'll send me next, but wherever it is will mean trouble. I could even get myself killed."

"You won't be," she'd said with more confidence than she felt, sitting with him in her Aunt Margaret's garden with rare English sunlight blazing all around them.

"My dear child"—he was ten years her senior—"I hope you're right. After this next assignment maybe I'll get one on which you can be with me. So let's wait awhile," he'd said, smiling at her, "before we produce beautiful redheaded babies. There's time for that. Meanwhile there's The Pill."

There was. Her aunt's doctor had equipped her with them, but she had not taken them; and she hadn't told Andy.

Once he'd said to her, "I've always avoided female redheads; stubborn, willful, bad-tempered, and enchanting. Look at me now, hopelessly hooked in about eleven minutes after meeting you."

At the Athens office he'd learned of his assignment and they'd flown back to London. She planned to return to her aunt's house before she went on home—if she did decide to go home. Her aunt, for whom she'd been named, had married late, a titled Englishman she'd met in New York. Ted Wilson was a widower with two grown children.

Meg, eighteen and in training when her aunt married, had been happy for her, desolate for herself. Her aunt had brought her up from the time she was four, her parents having died in a car crash.

I'll feel closer to Andy, she thought, if I remain in England and with someone of my own. She would inquire as to the proper procedures so that she could work there. But she hadn't inquired, because she had learned she was pregnant.

In a letter to Andy she'd said, "I won't say I'm sorry because I'm not, though I know how you feel."

He wrote as soon as her letter reached him. He remarked philosophically that The Pill didn't always work, he supposed, and now she must go back to the States and be with his mother. The boy—he was sure it would be a boy . . . "I hope he looks just like you though, darling"—must grow up where his father had grown up.

So she had come home, despite Aunt Margaret's pleadings and those of Ted Wilson. Andy had wanted his son to be born in the United States. Perhaps she would have considered disregarding Andy's wishes if she had not felt so guilty.

Andy had been practical. She had been stupid—and willful. Why, she did not really know. Perhaps, she thought much later, because I was a romantic? But in the nineteen-sixties she must have been feeble-minded not to have waited.

Yet if she had waited, if she had docilely taken the pill, as Andy believed she had, there would have been no small Andrew. Perhaps she had been more than just nightmarishly afraid that something would happen to Andy; perhaps she'd known it. Aunt Margaret had always said there was a fey streak, the Welsh, the Scotch ancestry, in the family.

So Meg had come home to Cornelia, the stranger who erected no barriers, except that one time when she had expressed herself definitely on the haste—"no more time than the law allowed"—in which Meg had been married. She couldn't understand Andy, she'd said. He could have given his mother time to be present. Meg was quite certain that Cornelia counted on her fingers, probably resigning herself to a big, healthy "premature" grandchild. But small Andrew had been properly born after his mother had carried him for a respectably long nine months.

7

Meg thought, driving between the big stone gate posts and up the avenue of great maples: I wonder if she'd give me two dollars—maybe it's more now—and a new suit?

She put the car in the garage in its accustomed place. When, six months after Andrew's birth, she had applied for and obtained an administrative position in the hospital, Cornelia had given her the car, and had recently decided it was about time to turn it in for a new one. Meg walked to the house. It was after five. Cornelia was home, her car was in. She would have had a romp with her grandchild and returned him to Clara who had charge of him and would be having tea alone; there were no parked cars by the house.

She would probably give me a lot more than two dollars plus an entire wardrobe, Meg thought, if I'd just go quietly and let her keep Andrew.

The front door was open, and Meg went into the wide hall, through the living room, and out to the big stone-floored, screened porch. There was a terrace beyond that, then a swimming pool.

She was in uniform and Cornelia, reading a novel and drinking iced tea on a fine summer's day, raised an eyebrow slightly. Had there been guests, Meg would have gone to her room, removed her lingering hospital taint, and changed before seeing Cornelia's friends. Cornelia preferred it. She also preferred that Meg change before she went to see Andrew, not that she feared Andrew's mother would waltz in with an infection as a gift for him, but because this was, or should be, customary. One came home from school, or work, and made oneself presentable. Cornelia had no objection to Meg's working, she believed that every able-bodied woman should usefully occupy her time and not waste her education—in Meg's case, university, nursing school, and Master's degree. Naturally, Meg didn't have to work, but, Cornelia said, to Meg and to her own friends, she'd be happier. It had nothing to do with earning. Andy had left his wife his insurance, which was about all he'd had to leave, and there was enough in Cornelia's portfolio, and various holdings—she was a major stockholder in the factory—to support half a dozen daughters-in-law, to say nothing of a dozen grandchildren. When Meg had said—timidly for her—that she'd like to contribute something, however little, to the household for herself and Andrew, Cornelia had been wounded, but kind. She'd said that Meg's attitude was commendable, "But except for what I've left the hospital, church, and my other charities, the annuities for the Mortons and Clara and a few small bequests, everything I have would have been Andy's and now of course will be his son's."

Now Meg said, "I'm sorry I'm late, Nana."

She could not have called her Cornelia nor would Cornelia have permitted it; or, mother; only one person had the right to call Cornelia mother and he was dead and buried beside his father in the Melton-Brand family plot. So Meg had called her mother-in-law "Mrs. Brand" until Cornelia had said, "We must find something else." Once Andrew was born, it was easy. "He won't be able to say grandmother for some time. How about Nana?"

Now Cornelia smiled brilliantly. She said, "I was beginning to worry," and rang an unnecessary bell, just as Morton, whose wife was the cook, came out with fresh tea. "I suppose Mrs. Elgin kept you?"

"Yes," said Meg. For once it was true.

"Trouble?"

"No—just a discussion about a matter of policy."

Meg said very little to Cornelia of hospital matters. She had learned early that Cornelia gathered bits of information as a jackdaw trinkets; only, unlike the jackdaw, she used them.

Meg sat down in a big chaise and put up her feet, which, as usual, hurt. The tea was on the table beside her and Morton offered small sandwiches and cookies. She accepted, saying, "I'm starved. All I had was coffee on the run at my lunch hour."

Cornelia, looking at her, saw her son's widow and her grandson's biological mother, a small slender young woman with red-gold hair, short and curling; a young woman with a fine skin, good features, and startling blue eyes. Meg looked at her husband's mother and her child's grandmother and saw a handsome woman, taller than herself, but almost as slender; a woman with no discernible gray in her dark, beautifully arranged hair; a woman with brown eyes, a square jaw, and a controlled mouth.

Meg remembered the first day she'd seen her; when, feeling very ill and looking it, burdened with grief and pregnancy, with tension and shock, and the added sorrow of leaving her aunt, she had somehow stumbled from the plane into Cornelia Brand's arms and let her take over. Later, in the big house, oppressed by it, by Cornelia's mourning apparel and by her own loneliness, she had searched Cornelia's face for a trace of Andy's features, but had not found it.

He'd spoken of his mother often during their brief acquaintance and short marriage. It had seemed to her then, although she was not sure, that he had spoken with pride but not with any deep affection. How could one know? Later she might have known, but not then.

"She's not as formidable as she looks."

"Do you look like her, darling?"

"Not at all. I understand I'm like my father's people, skinny, a mile high, and scholarly."

"Scholarly!"

"Well, that's what they were, educators, curators and such. Ma's early ancestors were farmers, and accumulated land. It was my grandfather Melton who built the house and factory. Maybe I'm a little like him, raw-boned, blond, big feet. I haven't the remotest idea who Ma looks like, although there's a dim primitive portrait of an ancestress with the same shaped face and dark eyes."

Young Andrew didn't look like his father, Cornelia had said, when Meg came home from the hospital. He looked like his grandfather. The portrait in the library and many photographs proved it. The baby did have a quiff of red-gold hair, which of course he'd inherited from Meg, but the rest of him was Brand. "Your eyes are blue," said Cornelia, "but so were Andy's, and the baby's are set just like his grandfather's."

Now they talked a little. Cornelia had had two committee meetings and had lunched with Anne Pearson at the Inn. There was talk of a strike at the factory. The reason was beyond Cornelia's grasp. The men and women who worked there had good wages, overtime, many fringe benefits, and decent homes; also the Melton public schools were among the best in the state. "Greed," said Cornelia, "and rabble rousers."

She added that she hoped by the time young Andrew was old enough to take over, things would have altered for the better, but she doubted it. "The best years have been behind us," she said, "since the First World War."

Later she reminded Meg that the Duffs were coming for dinner, so Meg got to her feet and went up to shower. In a robe, she looked in at Andrew who had his own nursery suite. His bedroom was next to Meg's with no connecting door, then his play room, and Clara's quarters—bedroom and small living room.

Andrew had had his supper and was running around in his night things. Clara Peabody, who had been with the Brands since Andy, Jr., was born, sat in a big chair, knitting. She looked up when Meg came to the door.

"Hi, Meg," she said, and the baby echoed cheerfully, "Hi, Meg."

Clara had come young to the Brands as a trained baby nurse. Once Andy had said of her, "The whole damned place would fall apart without her," and in the letter which had eventually put Meg on the plane to New York, "You can trust our baby to Clara."

She had done so, and by now she would have trusted Clara with her own life as well. After Andy had gone away to school Clara had stayed on and become essential to Cornelia. She was half secretary, untrained but efficient, and half housekeeper. The Mortons looked after the cooking and serving, housemaids came and went, and teams came to do heavy cleaning. Clara hired and fired, made out menus, ran special errands in the car Cornelia provided, and rarely took a day off. Her actual position was ambiguous. She dined with Meg and Cornelia when there were no guests. Otherwise she had her lunch and dinner upstairs with Andrew. She called Cornelia "Mrs. Brand." She called Meg "Meg," but only when they were alone. "For heaven's sake," Meg had said crossly, during the first months, "can't you call me Meg?"

"I'd be bounced."

"I doubt it. Andy loved you, Clara; he wanted us to be friends."

And they were.

"Bad day?" Clara asked, as Meg sat down on the floor and held out her arms to her son, who grinned at her, ignored the gesture, and went over to a toy box in which he rooted busily until he unearthed a soiled rabbit with one ear missing.

"Only moderately. How about you?"

"Routine. I wish you'd get out more, Meg."

Clara thought: I'm more than old enough to be her mother, and I wish I were.

"I get out."

"Not by yourself, you don't. You ought to be with friends your own age, and both sexes."

"I haven't made friends really, except at the hospital. I do see them occasionally."

They had their own people, their friends, and activities; I'm always the odd one out, Meg thought. And besides there was so little time. She worked, she came back to the Brand house.

Here she had met Cornelia's friends. After Andrew's birth, there'd been dinner parties here and elsewhere, concerts, summer theater, bridge, and the Country Club if a tennis match coincided with one of Meg's days off. More recently she'd gone to dinner at the Club and danced with the husbands of Cornelia's friends, or with someone's unattached house guest.

"Bunny!" cried Andrew, clutching his disreputable toy. He came to his mother, inviting her admiration. Meg kissed him and he said, "Kiss Bunny."

She did so and Clara said, "Put Bunny back in the box, Andrew."

"No."

"Then bring him to me."

He did so, holding the animal with desperation. He did not cry, he rarely cried. "Best child in the world," Cornelia often said. "I remember what a monster Andy was at his age. Clara remembers too."

Now he clambered into Clara's lap and said urgently, "Bunny's mine."

Clara held him carelessly. She was marvelous with him; she never hammered anything home, neither discipline, nor affection; everything was there like the air he breathed.

Clara said, "Of course he's yours." She added to Meg, "I try to keep him from inflicting Bunny on Mrs. Brand. Once or twice she's tossed it out, and I've retrieved it. I tell her he'll outgrow it."

The baby was almost asleep. Clara said softly, "She was with him almost an hour this afternoon."

"He pays very little attention to me," Meg said without bitterness.

Clara freed a hand, and brushed her thick gray hair from her forehead. She said, "He's not with you much, Meg. But he knows you belong to him."

Meg said, "I hope so," and smiled. She thought: Belong?

I look in on him before I go to work and when I get back. The days I'm off we have some time together. His grandmother comes like a window opening, or a treat. She's the goody at the end of the day. Clara is his real life.

She was not jealous of Clara. The little boy had never been ill except with the usual childish complaints. So Meg had never needed to sweep everyone else out and take charge. Clara was competent to handle practically everything anyway. She fulfilled Andrew's needs; she represented security. Cornelia represented excitement. She did not discipline him any more than she had his father. ("I was rotten spoiled," Andy had said.) Clara had been Andy's slide rule for behavior, and was now his son's. Cornelia was bright charming adventure. Clara was a rock.

What am I? Meg wondered. She kissed the top of her son's head, smiled at Clara and went back to her room.

If she were to take Andrew away, she could support him, but with whom would he be left in his formative years while she worked? Unless Clara would come too. But Clara could not. She had an old mother in a nursing home. Mrs. Peabody had every comfort. For years Clara had had a good salary, saved much of it, and maintained her mother's little house. Then there came a choice. Either Clara must give up her job and take care of her mother, or her mother must go into a home, and good ones cost the earth.

Cornelia had selected the home. Clara could not afford it, but Cornelia could—and did—in order to keep Clara.

Two

THE GERALD DUFFS were new in town. "New" meant anything from two weeks to twenty years. In the Duffs' case it had been four months. He was a young executive with a Midwestern firm, transferred now to the East, as regional sales manager in his company's Melton office. They'd rented a moderately old house in a good section and Cornelia had been introduced to Betsey Duff at a Garden Club meeting. Cornelia had been favorably impressed and had told Meg that the Duffs would be an addition. Newcomers were sometimes subtractions.

Dressing for dinner, Meg reflected further upon her relationship with her son. She loved him deeply, as an extension of Andy and for himself as an emerging individual. Illogically she felt she was more responsible for him than Andy had been and sometimes when she was bone tired and beset with uncertainty, she wondered if now Andy knew of her deception.

Brushing her curly cap of hair she thought: Andrew accepts me. But she knew she could not give him the balloon-going-up excitement his grandmother bestowed, or the comfort, consolation, and guardianship Clara provided. She was not resentful. This situation was of her own making. Blind with sorrow, shaken by uncertainty, and following Andy's directions, she had walked into a velvet-lined trap.

To separate the little boy from these surroundings, especially from Clara, would be unthinkable; yet, Meg thought about it every day, considering, planning, discarding, reconsidering. Alone with him in another city or state—she was qualified to work in a number of states—managing on her salary, and what she'd saved, she would have to stretch all she could earn to include rent, living expenses, and expert care for Andrew while she was working.

Andy's insurance, on Cornelia's advice, was safely invested at four percent. The income was minuscule, but if Andy's son ever needed the capital, the bonds could be sold. There'd be no other income except her take-home salary.

Meg's education had been financed by insurance policies her parents had carried, which also had seen her through her childhood, supplemented by her aunt whose earnings were substantial. The post-graduate degree and Meg's living expenses in the apartment she shared with two graduate students had been underwritten by her aunt. Formerly, after taking a B.S. and R.N., one could work days and study nights, but at the time Meg was taking her Master's, the rules had been changed. She had considered omitting the extra year of study, but Margaret Wilson had insisted, by telephone and air mail. She'd said, "It's necessary to your future. Ted and I will see you through and once you've accomplished this, you'll come to us for a visit."

Before that visit she'd seen her aunt and Ted Wilson three times since their marriage; twice they'd flown over on business, and at her graduation they'd come to be with her.

Meg was often painfully homesick for her brisk no-nonsense aunt, who had so long been her sole security and for the quiet Englishman of whom she was very fond. Margaret Wilson was an essential part of Meg's life. She thought with longing of the house in England, of Margaret and Ted and Ted's grown children, and would have given anything if she and Andrew could be there with them all.

Now and then Cornelia would ask, "Have you heard

from Lady Margaret? How is she?" It was natural for Cornelia to speak of the Wilsons and also to stress, without being obvious, that Ted's title was inherited, a baronetcy not a knighthood. To do Cornelia justice Meg believed that she herself was not impressed, but that in effect she was providing Meg with a background. Andrew, of course, being both a Melton and Brand needed no more than that.

Margaret Wilson wrote regretfully that they couldn't come over, although yearning to. They had never seen Andrew nor met Mrs. Brand, but travel allowances were small unless Ted was on business. "Can't you take a month off?" she'd asked, a while back, "and persuade Mrs. Brand to bring you and small Andrew to us?"

Meg hadn't tried; she was too deeply in Cornelia's debt, but sometimes Cornelia herself mentioned the possibility. "One of these summers you'll get a decent holiday—Betty Elgin gets a month, doesn't she?—and then we'll fly to your aunt's with Clara and the baby."

Clara, hearing of this possibility, said she was scared stiff of flying, but if Andrew flew, she would.

Meg was a little late getting downstairs because, having heard Andrew singing to himself in his tuneless happy fashion, she'd looked in on him and he'd informed her from his crib that Bunny thought she was pretty.

The Duffs had already arrived, Morton was mixing drinks, and Cornelia said brightly, "Oh, there you are, dear," and made the introductions to the Duffs, a good-looking couple, short woman, tall man and said, "My son's widow, Meg."

It was always that way, never "my daughter," or "my daughter-in-law." Either would have to be explained, but "my son's widow" was self-explanatory. Any stranger could learn, in the town or in this house, when, where, and how.

Sometimes, lying awake, Meg thought of Ruth and Naomi and reflected that there was no Boaz for Naomi to recommend.

Now it appeared that the Duffs came complete with

children, a boy of six, a girl of three. As Andrew was almost three, Meg and Betsey Duff talked babies. At one point, Cornelia, accepting her second very dry martini—she allowed herself two every evening—remarked that, in reality, Meg's knowledge of children was eighty percent academic, and explained that this had been gained through her training. "But now that she's toiling at our local hospital—Have you seen it, Mrs. Duff? We're very proud of it—Clara and I take over." She then explained Clara.

Meg flushed through her slight tan; she never tanned deeply, most redheads don't, they burn; so she was careful, with the result that her creamy skin was merely sun-gilded. She said lightly, "Like a tired businessman, I get home in time to enjoy Andrew, but only for a little while. I've often considered working nights."

"Ridiculous," said Cornelia.

Gerald Duff remarked that he and Meg were in the same category, although now and then he did sneak home early.

"To get in a round of golf," his wife commented.

But their boy was older; he could stay up later than Andrew. In the autumn he'd be going to school. His father said, "I'll have to brush up on my homework," and Betsey said, "I wish I could see little Andrew, I'm hooked on babies."

"Control your addiction," her husband advised, "for at least a little while."

Cornelia said pleasantly that Andrew would be sleeping and Clara didn't encourage visitors. "She's a tartar," she added, "but do come for tea someday soon, Mrs. Duff. I usually manage to spend an hour or more with Andrew around that time, so you'd see him. Of course, I think he's well worth seeing."

At dinner—planned by Clara, cooked by Mrs. Morton, served by Morton—the conversation skimmed around the town. The Duffs were properly enthusiastic. They loved their house. "Even," said Gerald, "at the fantastic rent. We don't want to buy or build yet. It's incredible the way super-numeraries like me are bounced around. Betsey and I have been married for eight years and we've moved four times, courtesy of the firm."

It was a big company, and had offices all over. He told Cornelia that the main plants were on the West coast; he and Betsey had been born and brought up in San Francisco.

Cornelia said that once San Francisco had been her favorite city, next to Boston. "Beautiful," she added, "and stimulating, I even like the fog. But"—she made a face—"I was last there some years ago, when I made a world cruise. It had changed."

"You should see it now," said Gerald.

The talk drifted to the Country and Garden clubs, and to the Village Beautification and Preservation Guild, founded over a hundred years ago. "There was another Johnson in the White House then," Cornelia reminded them. She added that the Guild could always use volunteer help, as could the hospital, library, and the Historical Society. "If Meg didn't insist on working, she'd be my right hand," she added regretfully.

Meg recalled how enthusiastic Cornelia had been when Meg had wondered, aloud, if there would be a place for her in the hospital.

Betsey Duff felt a slight shift in the wind direction, and said, without regret, that she hadn't much time for outside activities, with the house, kids, and marketing. "But I'll try to attend the Garden Club meetings," she assured her hostess, "hoping my thumb will come all over green."

Cornelia smiled and said, "Well, if you're able to give us a few hours after your boy starts school, I know several baby sitters, middle-aged and responsible." Since the Duffs attended her church, which provided a nursery for the small children of its congregation, she asked how they liked the minister?

They said they liked Mr. Jones and that he and his wife had called on them shortly after their arrival in Melton. "I understand he's a newcomer himself," Gerald said.

"Such an addition," said Cornelia, repressing any mention of Mr. Jones's unfortunately modern and self-willed predecessor.

From the ministry the conversation slid into medicine. It appeared that Dr. Scott had been recommended to the Duffs and he, in turn, had recommended a good pediatrician, of whom Cornelia approved, and who looked after Andrew. "A clever, personable young man," said Cornelia.

Betsey Duff said that in her opinion Dr. Scott was a living doll.

"Which one?" inquired Meg.

They'd been recommended to the older, Gerald explained. "But I understand the son has taken over most of the practice. Betsey was talking about the son. She has a weakness for young good-looking doctors."

"Who hasn't?" asked Cornelia and went on to say, "I hardly know Charles now, but I knew him as a child. I grew up with his father, Bill Scott; he's a little older than I and I was madly in love with him before he went off to school, and even for a while after. His wife is an old friend of mine."

Well, well, thought Meg.

"Then you're one of his old patients?" said Gerald. "I don't mean in years."

Cornelia laughed. "Originally, yes," she said, "but later I became a patient of Dr. Foster's—an excellent internist."

Younger, too, Meg thought and a dedicated apple polisher, which William Scott wasn't. To him such apples were wormy. His patients loved him and so did the students, nurses, and staff.

She left the dining room mentally, thinking of Charles. She was astonished at herself. She had not believed she

would ever again conjure up the faintest interest in men—
or a particular man—although that of course was absurd and
would be abnormal.

The Duffs went home early, their sitter was sixteen and
her parents had a rule about late hours. Cornelia knew the
parents and was certain that the child—Cynthia, was it?—
was responsible. Responsibility ran in the family. Cynthia's
father was a carpenter often employed by Cornelia, and her
mother a paid aide at the hospital.

When the Duffs had said good night, Cornelia stood
with Meg at the foot of the stairs.

"Are you coming up, Nana?"

"No, I've mail to attend to." Cornelia had a small sunny
room, which she called an office. There she talked to
strangers and consulted with Clara, investigated appeals,
answered personal mail, and spent some time on the telephone. She added, "The Duffs appear to be a very nice
couple."

Meg agreed.

"Perhaps you can see something of them? It's good for
you to be with young people, outside of your work. I feel
you're terribly restricted, the hospital all day and after that
an old woman and a baby."

Cornelia didn't think of herself as an old woman, nor
was she, and Meg didn't believe in the admixture of con-
sideration and pathos which Cornelia sometimes displayed,
yet it always affected her against her better judgment. One
thing Andy had certainly inherited from his mother was
charm; another, a sense of timing.

His was a different charm of course and male; it had
melted Meg's bones. Cornelia was plausible, but Andy had
been honest; he'd been honest as a reporter, as a husband and
lover. She had known him so short a time that she often
wondered how accurate her evaluation had been.

From their first encounter she had always seen Andy

surrounded by light—in crowded rooms in London, with the
noise and the smoke and rain falling steadily outside; at the
Wilsons' house, in or out of doors, under blue sky or gray,
always that light; and in Greece where the sun was dazzling
and brilliant, a clarity of light incredible to her. Andy always
maintained his own radiance. There were flaws to be sure;
she saw them faintly through this light, but who had none?
Perhaps she would have found more if there'd been time,
but would she ever have found anything less than endearing?
She recognized, in Greece, the slight touch of arrogance and
had needled him about it. She'd said, "You were a buccaneer
or a tremendous milord in another incarnation, a sort of
off-with-his-head personality," and he'd laughed with her
and remarked, "That's a legacy from Mom."

That was true, she knew now, but while Cornelia's
arrogance also had some charm, it was not endearing. But
then Cornelia wasn't Andy.

Her aunt Margaret had been completely dismayed when
Meg had announced, after the first weekend Andy spent with
them, that they were to be married as soon as possible.

"But you scarcely know him," she'd said, and Ted Wilson
had shaken his distinguished head and advised, "Take it
slowly, Meg; it's early on."

The Wilsons liked Andy; he was attractive to most people,
physically and mentally. But Meg was passionately in love
for the first time; she knew it was for the first time—that
other emotional involvement didn't count.

Andy liked the things she liked: people, discussions,
music. He had, she learned, a quick, rather bawdy wit;
professionally he liked tough assignments. He was exciting
and fun to be with. He also had great sensitivity and was a
patient, imaginative lover. Meg, having no basis for comparisons, did not know how skillful he was; she was simply
grateful for him, for love and fulfillment.

"I'll probably drag you all over this wretched planet when

22

things are so you can follow, or not be too damned far away, you poor benighted infant."

Even had Andy lived, she could not have gone where he was, unless his Saigon assignment had been over before Andrew was born.

Assumption and speculation—all fruitless. If they'd had ten years, five, even two, so she might have really known him, beyond the Biblical sense of the word, beyond the beginnings of the mental relationship. . . .

"My God, I'm ten years older than you. I'll be an old man in twenty years and you'll still be a redheaded witch!"

On the following day, Meg went to the hospital coffee shop for a midmorning snack and Charles Scott, wandering over to the table where she was sitting with one of the charge nurses, murmured, "If you don't mind, girls . . . ," dragged a chair out with his foot and sat down. He put his dark head in his hands. "I've had it," he announced. "Up most of the night. How my old man has taken it all these years I'll never know. Nor how he waited that long for his heart attack. I look for mine about a week from Tuesday."

Meg and her companion commiserated with him with marked insincerity and presently, when the other woman left, Charles smiled at Meg and said, "Hi."

He was a medium tall, spare man with an infectious grin and a sort of—what was it?—mischief, sparkle, which found its way through his evident and valid fatigue. Meg knew that he was hard working and well liked. Mrs. Elgin had once said of Charles Scott, "It will take Melton—the older generation that is—a long time to accept him as a one hundred percent successor to his father." And had added that she, of course, had been born in a very different sort of town—in fact, New York.

Charles drank his coffee, said something very impolite about it, and lit a cigarette. "I advise my patients not to smoke. Apparently you don't, which is courageous of you."

"I never liked it," Meg told him.

"Well, bully for you. When's your next day off?"

She answered, startled, that unless a crisis arose she would be off Sunday.

"Splendid. How about dragging our tired old bodies around the Country Club dance floor Saturday night?"

"I don't believe——"

"Try," Scott said, interrupting. "If you discipline yourself to believe six impossible things before breakfast, you'll have no difficulty, midmorning."

He then looked at her and said thoughtfully, "The uniform is becoming to you as it is to most women, even plain women. But I'd admire to see you out of disciplined white. Don't tell me you have to stay home with Aunt Cornelia— I used to call her that once—or even with your infant. I know all about Clara Peabody," said Dr. Scott, yawning frankly. "I know all about everybody, almost."

She said, "How nice. Do people consult you as a reference book—Who's Who Dun and Bradstreet?"

"Also police blotter," he agreed. "How about Saturday?"

"I'll think about it."

"You do just that, but not for too long. There are dozens of gorgeous, man-hungry Melton girls who would grasp at even this weary straw. Some of them are rich, and it never hurts a rising young physician to be seen with a rich girl, particularly at the altar. How often I've berated my mother, who was just a poor, pretty nurse when my father crashed into her in a corridor. She should have stood at someone else's bedside and he should have married Cornelia Brand née Melton." He shook his head, rose, said gently, "I knew Andy very well, Meg—I'd like to know his wife and son." He stretched, said, "Blow me to coffee, will you? I left my money in my other white coat. I'll call you," he added, and was on his way even before he heard himself called on his pocket page.

"Well, really!" said Meg aloud.

That evening at dinner she told Cornelia, "Dr. Scott has asked me to go to the dance with him Saturday."

"Charles, I assume?" said Cornelia, adding pleasantly, "Why don't you? It will be a change." But her left eyebrow was somewhat elevated. In astonishment or displeasure?

Meg thought: I can make up my own mind. I'm not afraid of her. And she wasn't. She'd been on her own for some time before she met Andy Brand. Yet, Cornelia could make her feel uncomfortable.

"Perhaps I shall," she said.

"Did he ask you for dinner?"

"Why—that is I don't know. He's going to telephone."

"If he's anything like his father, even if you do dine with him," Cornelia said, "he'll be called away in the middle of the soup. Helen, Charles's mother, was accustomed to uncertain meals, broken engagements, or being left high, if not dry, at someone's house, or her own, or the Club."

Meg said, "I'm just going to dance with Dr. Scott, Nana. I'm not planning to marry him."

Her tone was a trifle sharp, but Cornelia's was smooth when she answered, "I didn't think you were, dear."

Later over coffee in the living room Cornelia talked about Andrew. "Have you noticed how much more he's talk ing? I thought he was rather slow. Andy was talking a blue streak at this age." So, by easy stages, Cornelia's conversation became centered about her son and eventually she said, "There was never anyone like Andy, except, of course, his father."

Meg went to her room in a state of exasperation. Cornelia hadn't said, "I don't think you should go out alone with a man." Such a comment would have been the height of absurdity and Cornelia was never absurd, but her rejection of the idea was implicit.

Before Andrew's birth Cornelia had spoken to Meg about

Andy's father. She'd said, "I was a young woman when he died; I had a number of opportunities to remarry and to give Andy a father. . . . Perhaps I should have, but I couldn't."

Andrew Senior's widow could not; Andrew Junior's widow should not.

It was a warm night, soft and fragrant. Meg, after her quiet inspection of Andrew Third in his crib, went to bed and could not sleep. The windows stood wide, a small disheartened breeze stirred fitfully. She had not turned on her air conditioning. Now she did so, shut the windows, and pulled up a summer blanket. Andy had been, she believed, a reasonable man. He would not wish her to remain here, year in year out, adapting and compliant, with no life of her own beyond these walls and hospital corridors. He would not want her to wear mourning forever, even in her heart. He'd want her to laugh, to come alive, and even to love again.

"How about past lovers?" he'd asked her, on that little Greek island.

"None."

"I'm to believe that?"

"Yes." Then she had laughed, sitting there on a beach, deserted except for themselves with the hot sunlight blazing in her hair. "Well, one almost," she had admitted.

"What do you mean 'almost'?"

"When I was taking my post-grad studies, he was just about through his internship and going into the service. But," said Meg, "I'm the marrying kind."

"And he wasn't?"

"Not then, anyway. I've no idea what he did later. But young interns just couldn't afford marriage unless they had tons of family money or the girls had. He didn't have, nor did I."

Andy had reached out and ruffled her hair. "It should burn my fingers," he'd told her, "but it doesn't. . . . So that's that, Mrs. Brand."

26

"Not altogether," she'd told him honestly. "I shared an apartment, but the other girls weren't always there. It became a temptation, Andy. I believed I was in love and I was on my own. I daresay the thought of Aunt Margaret and the way she brought me up was a restraint, if I can say something so outmoded. Anyway, I was scared and I'm glad I was."

But Andy was asleep on the curving beach, hat tilted over his eyes, so she sat there under the striped umbrella, her hands around her golden knees, looking at the infinitely blue sky, the infinitely blue water and as much of this small island's coast as she could see. She forgot Keith Lansing. She forgot everything but this island, which she and Andy spoke of as their own, despite a hotel and tourists. She forgot everything but how happy she was and how much she desired this moment to last forever. . . .

Now, in another place and at another time, she put her face against a pillow, conscious that she wanted to cry for no reason other than that the past is always a part of the present.

Three

YOU LOOK very pretty, Meg," Cornelia commented agreeably before dinner on Saturday evening. Clara had said so, too, when Meg had stopped in to see Andrew after he was in bed. Andrew had also been complimentary. He'd consulted his rabbit, "Meg's pretty," he said, "isn't she?" Then he looked at his mother, "Bunny thinks so too," he told her again.

Clara said, "He has an eye for the girls, like his father." She added resignedly, "I've given up trying to make him call you Mommie."

"It's all right as long as he knows I'm his mother," Meg said, "and Mommie I don't much care for."

"Well, he's right. That dress becomes you. Will you tell Mrs. Brand I'll be down presently?"

Meg went down for cocktails. Clara said she would follow. She did not drink except on special occasions—birthdays, Christmas, and New Year's.

Meg's dress was white but not the disciplined white against which Charles had warned her. It was a cotton frock, short, scooped out at the neck, and sleeveless. She wore her big aquamarine engagement ring over her wedding ring; tonight she had added the rest of the aquamarines, Andy's wedding present: necklace, earrings, and a slender bracelet. She took a little aquamarine-colored sweater downstairs with her.

Cornelia, regarding her, reflected that the present fashions, even those on the conservative side, were a trifle girlish for a widow, however young, but admitted that at least the hemline wasn't above the knee—not that the junior Mrs. Brand hadn't good knees.

Meg delivered Clara's message, which was when Cornelia told her that she looked very pretty, to which Meg said, pleased, "Why, thank you, Nana."

Clara appeared presently and when they went in to dinner the conversation was general and mostly about Andrew. Clara declined coffee in the living room, said casually to Meg, "Remember me to Charles; I'd like to see him again," and went back upstairs.

The living room was large and comfortable; a few ancestors looked down benevolently from pale green walls, the furniture was old and shining; there were ample chairs, love seats, end tables, and ash trays. On either side of the fireplace, book shelves, with here and there a piece of porcelain or ivory instead of a book—just enough things to arouse interest, but no clutter.

"Too bad Charles couldn't take you to dinner," said Cornelia, "not that the Club food is imaginative."

"I really didn't expect that he could get away," Meg said.

When he had called to ask, "How about it?" and she'd said, "Yes," he'd added without apology, "I can't make it early. I'll pick you up about nine."

He came a little after nine, greeting Morton, and following him into the living room, "Hello, Aunt Cornelia," he said, as if he'd seen her day before yesterday.

Cornelia said, "How nice to see you, Charles. May Morton give you coffee before you take off?"

He accepted the delicate Chelsea demitasse, refusing cream or sugar, sitting there by Cornelia, his long legs extended. He looked about him, sampling the strong black brew. "It's been a long time," he remarked, "but the room hasn't changed. Oh, I've no doubt the paint and chintzes are new, but essentially no change."

Cornelia said, "I'm glad you remember it," and did not add that change distressed her. "How is your father?" she asked.

"Screaming the house down because he finds it hard to accept the advice he so often gives to others, which is relax, cut down, take it easy. Therefore most of the practice is in the incompetent hands of his only son."

"Nonsense," said Cornelia briskly. "I'm certain you're most capable."

"I'd love to prove it to you," Charles said with a gleam in his eyes. "Not of course that I wish you a pox or a murrain." He rapped the table beside him. "*Unberufen,*" he added.

Cornelia's expression was unreadable, but Meg was conscious of a curious hostile undercurrent.

"And your mother?" asked Cornelia. "I haven't seen Helen in some time."

"Mom's fine. She's currently in California with Sal." He turned to Meg. "Sally's my young sister," he told her; "married, and with two kids. Well, now she has four. Mom went out to be with her during the arrival of number three, who turned out to be twins. She wouldn't let Dad go along; she was afraid he'd fire Sally's obstetrician. He may go out to bring Mom home if they let him fly."

"Twins!" said Cornelia. "How exciting. I'm sure your mother has been of incalculable help."

Charles set down his cup. He said, "Well, Sally seems to think so." He rose and said to Meg, "How about joining the station-wagon set, and following my old-fashioned lead? It's terrible," he added gloomily, "to be in the middle."

"In the middle of what?" asked Meg.

"Everything—too old to be a hippie, too young to be a really dependable square, and not old enough to try to swim with the minnows. I've been to the Club only two or three times since I came home. It was a gas, watching the contortions of infants and the attempts of their elders to emulate them. However, it's all money in the bank for those in my profession—the plodding G.P.'s, the orthopedic men, the osteopaths." He went, smiling, to Cornelia, said, "Thanks for letting me borrow Meg," and stood aside for Meg to precede him. She said goodnight to her mother-in-law who reassured her, "Clara, Andrew, and I will hold the fort. Have a good time, dear. . . . Good night, Charles."

In the hall Meg vanished into the powder room and Charles talked with Morton. "How's your wife?" he wanted to know.

"Just fine," said the old man. "Thank you, Mr.—that is Dr. Charles."

"And you, old chum?"

"I can't complain. There's no cure for growing old. Mrs. Morton doesn't have that problem yet, being younger."

He never referred to her, nor did Cornelia, by her given name. When Meg first came to the Brand house, she doubted that Mrs. Morton had one and asked Clara, who said, "I hate to tell you because it doesn't suit her. It's Gwendolyn."

"Sorry to be so long," said Meg, emerging from the powder room. "I'd eaten off my lipstick." She thought: I hope Cornelia told Morton not to wait up. I wouldn't dare.

On the steps she said, "I was afraid to repair my face and wash my hands while you were still with Nana."

"Nana!"

"Oh, she's taught Andrew to call her that; he can't manage Grandma yet."

"Why afraid?"

She said frankly, "I don't think you like each other much."

"Of course we don't," he admitted cheerfully as they walked toward his car, "although once upon a time I thought my adopted auntie a royal personage, and she spoiled me only a grade below Andy."

In the car he asked, "What hour is curfew?"

She said lightly, "None imposed. Why should there be?"

"I dunno, except that Aunt Cornelia often puts me in mind of many women—and some men—who believe they're really made in the Lord's image. Remember preserving thy going out and coming in? Only for preserving read watching over?"

"Nana," said Meg, "has begun to realize that I'm comparatively adult."

Driving through the soft, dark night, trimmed only with stars, Meg noticed idly how smoothly he drove, his hands firm and easy on the wheel. She thought of Andy—although she had not often been with him in a car—how reckless a driver yet how miraculously safe, laughing at her when she cautioned him. "I won't have a wifely back- or front-seat driver, darling. Relax."

"But you take such chances."

"Don't all of us, one way or another? Look at you, marrying a stranger."

Charles was talking to her; she forced her attention back from another year, another country, another man, and said, "I'm sorry——"

"You weren't listening."

"No. I was a hundred years and thousands of miles away."

"I daresay you often are," he said quietly. "I was saying I'm sorry you were perceptive enough to realize your Nana and I are not exactly devoted."

"Why sorry?"

"Because I intend coming around to the stately home as often as I can—to see you, meet your son, and renew an old friendship with Clara Peabody. Now the situation might make you feel uncomfortable."

"No," said Meg after a moment, "it won't."

"Actually," said Charles, "while I have on my white-coated shoulder a small chip which she put there, I didn't

32

mind seeing her. She was so much a part of my growing up —amusing to be with in a regal sort of way, and Andy's mother. Everything that belonged to Andy was fine with me!"

"Did you know his father?"

"Oh, sure," said Charles. "Very attractive man. He was killed early in World War Two as you must know. Andy and I were just kids. I came close to having a brother in Andy. He was a little older and I looked up to him. I patterned myself after him. He had more—well—I guess it was guts; he was an adventurer, a chance taker and a leader. I just tagged along."

She said, "I hadn't much time with him; we rarely talked about past things. He must have spoken of you to me, but he hadn't gotten around to talking of his childhood."

"Few things in my life have affected me as much as his death. I tried to write you a dozen times, but I can't express myself on paper. Andy could. He was tops."

"Yes," said Meg, her throat tight. She added, hesitantly, "What happened—to your friendship, I mean?"

"Nothing, if you mean between Andy and me. When he came home, I saw him, and sometimes in New York. When I heard he'd married, I hoped it would be right for him. He'd had some narrow escapes, and I don't mean in his profession."

"I know. He told me about them if not in detail."

"He would. . . . How come you landed here, Meg?"

She told him and he said, "Yes, he'd want you to be looked after and secure; and he'd want his kid to grow up in Melton."

She said, "But you don't approve."

"Do you operate on ESP? . . . Whether I do or not isn't the point. I see the logic, the practicality. In Andy's shoes I would have given you the same directive. It's just that his mother is a velvet hammer, a satin steamroller. . . . Sorry, I don't know you well enough to say that."

She remarked with spirit, "I can look after myself, Dr. Scott."

"Not Scotty, Mrs. Junior Brand? I call you Meg."

"I don't like Scotty."

"How about Charles? . . . Call me Charlie, and I'll clobber you."

As they turned into the Club driveway, he asked abruptly, "Why don't you then?"

"Why don't I what? You *do* have a grasshopper mind."

"Look after yourself, with the help of your English aunt."

"She's American," said Meg, "married to an Englishman. They both wanted me to stay there and I wanted to, actually. But everything was so—I can't explain it—unreal, confused; like walking on a strange road in a thick fog, knowing you're lost. And also Andy had told me what he wanted me to do."

"Yes." He thought that was taking advantage of a situation, but most men would. Andy was like his mother, an own-way-getter. Maybe it would have been better if Meg had stayed in England until she regained her emotional footing. Hell, he thought, I'm glad she didn't.

At the Club, pausing by tables, having people stop at theirs, Meg was aware of Charles Scott's popularity, particularly with young women aged eighteen to thirty.

He danced easily and Meg was conscious of the proximity of his body, which disturbed yet pleased her, for she had told herself after Andy died that no man would ever again attract her. Yet she'd known of course that one, or many, might. She was not stupid about sex; she was young and healthy and recognized response when she experienced it. She had not—until now—since the day she met Andy Brand.

Sex, with love and fulfillment, however brief with Andy; sex attraction with what she'd thought was love with Keith, prior to Andy—but no fulfillment, for which she'd thanked heaven after she'd met Andy. Before Keith, the usual forays and high-school flutters—sex awakened by natural curiosity and dusted with the mica of adolescent romance. During her hospital training she'd seen sex objectively in many of its aspects—frustrations, deviations—and also in its results. That had been sex in theory.

Her time with Andy had been so short that it was like caviar and wine—just enough nourishment to take the first edge from hunger. But she was convinced that if it had been given them to sit long together at the feast, it would have been wonderful, wholly satisfying, stilling all needs except theirs for each other.

"What are you thinking about?" Charles asked as they returned to their table for the simple club supper. "And how about a drink?"

She said she'd like one, long and cool and not too strong, and added truthfully that she'd been thinking about him.

"I don't dance that badly."

"You dance very well."

"Thanks. So what were you thinking?"

"Nothing specific. A woman usually thinks about her partner. How unflattering to you had I been thinking of Mrs. Elgin, or that recent dust-up in the pediatric ward, or even wondering if young Andrew is asleep which, knowing his capacity for relaxation and also knowing Clara, I'm sure he is."

"You weren't thinking only of me, Meg."

"Who has ESP now? No, of Andy, too."

He couldn't say, "Please, no comparisons." So he said, "I thought perhaps you were wondering about Nana and what *she's* thinking. Bet you a stethoscope to a scalpel she's busy modeling me in wax and looking for long sharp pins."

"Has she reason to?"

"Only her own, but you won't tell me all that was on your mind under that red hair."

"No." She gave him her slow, wide smile and his heart accelerated. He thought: Take it easy, Charlie. He didn't want anyone else to call him that, but he was informal with himself.

She said, "Perhaps I shouldn't ask—if so skip it—but

what happened between your family and the Brands? I don't mean you and Andy."

"What have you heard?" he asked cautiously.

"Nothing. I know only that your father was once Nana's physician."

"That he was, also her husband's, Andy's, and anyone else's in the household. But I don't know what happened."

She thought: He's lying. She conceded his right, shrugged her pretty shoulders, and said, "Forgive me for being indiscreet."

"The indiscreeter—is there such a word?—the better, honey, on certain levels."

"Nosy then," she said, smiling.

The drinks came, with little sandwiches and coffee, and the offer of ices in three flavors. And Meg said, "Okay, so I've been warned twice."

"How twice?"

"Oh, big, bad wolf, just now, and don't inquire into what doesn't concern you, a moment earlier."

"That's right." He laughed. "No wonder Andy fell in love with you. Oh, not just because of what you see in your mirror, though that's sufficient, but you're fun and likable as well; also very candid. He liked candor, Andy did."

"We were honest with each other," she told him, "from the beginning." She paused, thinking of the cocktail party where they'd met, the noisy room smelling of tobacco smoke, liquor, perfume. "That is as honest as two human beings can be. I suppose it's never really one hundred percent."

"No," said Charles, "but you're young to have discovered that. Tell me more about yourself, the people in England and all."

She did so briefly, adding, "You know all this already, at least the bare bones. Now it's your turn."

"Dull: birth, uneventful growing up, good family, schooling. Then an anxious intern, an overconfident intern, a hitch

36

in the Navy and home to settle down knowing a damned sight less than I once thought. I used to be pretty arrogant."

She said idly, "Andy was, in a way."

"Oh, his was a birthright, an inheritance. I copied it, probably because I felt inferior at first, and later, insecure."

She asked, "Are you happy here, Charles?"

"Of course. I like it. I know this place as I'd know a room I was born in and never left. I'm besotted about my parents. I admire my father even when he infuriates me. I'm not trying to fill his shoes; no one ever wears the same size and make as the other fellow. I like my work, though I'm not satisfied with it. I hope I can do a hell of a lot better, given time and the further education which comes with practice. I like most of my patients in varying degrees. When I can't help them, I pass them on to the specialists. I don't practice surgery, obstetrics, or psychiatry. I'm a G.P. which, while limited in scope, is getting rare. Maybe someday I'll announce that I'm an internist or whatever. Meantime, hospital, house calls, office—every day I learn a little more about people and medicine, I hope."

"You're a good doctor, Charles," Meg told him.

"I can't be yours," he said sadly. "Aunt Cornelia would never entrust you to my tender loving care."

"Maybe she won't have anything to say about it." Meg glanced at her watch, and added, "I'm sorry to suggest that it's time for me to go home. Tomorrow means church for me. It's probably just another day for you unless, like a lot of doctors, you spend it on the links."

"I'd rather go fishing, although I get seasick. I don't go often. Dad's patients are accustomed to having him available nights, days, and weekends. I have to go along with this brutal regime or be disinherited. Do you like to fish?"

"Yes, but I haven't had much opportunity in recent years."

"Then someday I'll take you and you can hold my head," he said cheerfully.

"How in the world did you get along in the Navy?"

"By not being on a ship. I was stationed on mother earth, in a mammoth stateside hospital. Okay, so let's go."

When they reached the house, Meg gave him the key, saying, "I hope Nana told poor Morton not to wait up."

The lights were on, the house quiet.

"Evidently she let him totter off to his couch."

"With some ambivalence perhaps," Meg said. "Naturally if I were to be late, she wouldn't want him waiting up; she's really considerate of her people. On the other hand, I'm certain the possibility of my coming in at any old hour would bother her."

He said, "It isn't very late." He pulled her toward him, kissed her lightly and released her. "Thank God Auntie herself isn't crouching in the shadows."

Meg said, "Good night, Charles, and thank you for a lovely evening."

"There will be others," said Charles. He turned at the door and looked at her shining hair, the slightly flushed face. He said, "Of course the last thing either of us should do is to become involved with each other."

"We're not involved," Meg said firmly.

Involvement meant something more than an evening at a country club or driving idly through a summer night. Involvement meant more than conversation, an exchange of dossiers or an idea or two, and more than a casual kiss at an evening's end.

"Not yet," said Charles, "but I'm willing to risk it if you are and even if you're not."

She laughed on a clear note of gaiety and Cornelia, reading in bed with the door open, heard it as one hears a faraway bell, laid aside her book, and looked at the clock.

She thought: I should have kept Morton up. . . . No, I should have stayed downstairs and offered Charles a drink when they came in. But Meg would have resented that, she thought further; she isn't a child.

Cornelia thought of the child asleep nearby. She was careful not to spend too much time with him and to spend it in the way a lavish hand scatters gold, making every moment exciting, unusual, something to which he'd look forward. Clara was always there; Meg came and went; but she, Cornelia, was a blaze of light across a quiet sky. She did not overtly spoil him, nor did she discipline. Clara disciplined, Meg did not, feeling that a child should not be on two leashes. But Cornelia believed Andrew's mother did not suspect there was a second leash; soft, but guiding.

She heard Meg come upstairs and called to her.

Meg stopped at Cornelia's open door. The room was suffused with becoming pink light and she leaned against a bed rest with a rosy bedjacket around her elegant shoulders. A book was beside her on the four poster, her reading glasses on the open pages.

"Did you have a good time?" Cornelia asked, smiling.

"Wonderful," said Meg, still flushed, her hair somewhat disheveled. By the wind through an open car window or something else?

Distaste rose in Cornelia's throat like bile. She said, "Come in a moment and sit down. You can sleep tomorrow. Did you see anyone we know?"

They had a short, pleasant conversation and then Cornelia said yawning, "Perhaps Charles can come for drinks sometime or lunch or dinner or whatever. He might like a swim. I suppose he told you he practically grew up here?"

"Yes." Meg went to the door. "Good night, Nana," she said, and Cornelia advised, "If you look in on Andrew, be very quiet. Clara had some difficulty in getting him to sleep."

"I won't disturb him," said Meg and felt a scratch of anxiety like an encounter with a thorn.

She made her way to Andrew's room; she opened his door softly. He was asleep. She could see the round curve of his cheek, and the rabbit clutched in one fat arm, and the tiny night light shedding reassurance.

In her mind, she kissed him and had started for her own room, when Clara came toward her like a substantial ghost in a gray dressing gown, her feet bare.

"Have fun?"

"Yes," said Meg. "Why are you awake?"

The little glow of the evening receded. She felt cross; Cornelia lying in her rosily lighted bed, Clara creeping down corridors.

"Heard you come in," said Clara.

"Mrs. Brand said Andy was restless and you had trouble with him."

"Oh?" Clara brushed her hair back from her forehead. She whispered, "He woke up once after you left. His grandmother went in and played with him for quite a while before he went back to sleep."

"I see," Meg smiled and touched the older woman's shoulder. She said, "Good night, Clara," and went on to her room.

She thought: So that was it. She also thought: I think Nana hates me and there's nothing I can do about it.

Kind, reasonable Cornelia; also implacable, devious Cornelia.

Four

M EG SLEPT FITFULLY, dreaming, waking up, sometimes half in tears, sometimes in terror as if the dream had been a nightmare. Once toward morning she found herself struggling out of bed, convinced that Andrew was in danger, and she must get to him. She stood there in her thin nightgown, her bare feet on the rug, and she was perspiring; the drops stood on her upper lip, at the edge of her hairline, and trickled down her back.

What had happened? Where was Clara?

In a moment, the panic passed and she was standing by the bed, alone in a room which, in her dream, had been filled with faceless menace; the windows were open, and the summer wind was cool, as it usually is near dawn.

Meg got back into bed not turning on the light, but groping her way between the sheets. She was not given to nightmares, but to nebulous dreams half remembered. She didn't remember this one, and was grateful for that; all she retained was a sense of threat and darkness. She told herself: "It couldn't have been the dinky little sandwiches at the Club, unless they were loaded with something unknown to me." Then she found herself thinking of Charles Scott and smiling, relaxed, drifted into deep, dreamless sleep.

She woke to bright sunlight, a hot day, and the sounds of Clara's voice and Andrew's in the corridor; she looked at the clock and realized that she had overslept. But it was permissible on her Sundays off; just as long as she was up and dressed in time to have breakfast with Cornelia, Andrew, and Clara, and then get ready for church and the rest of the routine day.

Winter, autumn, spring, and summer always church and the light sifting through stained glass and the Reverend Mr. Jones's undistinguished voice, delivering an undistinguished sermon which could affront no one. And after that, the ride to the cemetery, not far away. It was a beautiful cemetery on a hill, the headstones, monuments—there was a mausoleum on the Brand-Melton plot—well cared for, the grass tended and old trees trimmed. Meg hated every inch of the ground, but unless she was working or ill, she dutifully made the pilgrimage to watch Andrew. He had been permitted to come here ever since he could walk, happily oblivious of the significance of his surroundings, he admired the grass and the trees, and climbed on the white iron furniture. Only in severe snowstorms did Cornelia omit the ceremony. And in the kinder seasons she walked briskly about, regarded the various resting places, plucked weeds, and made mental notes if things were not all they should be.

It was absurd, it was morbid . . . No, Cornelia was neither absurd nor morbid. It was almost, Meg reflected, as if she took a certain satisfaction in making certain where people were, parents, grandparents, Andrew senior, Andrew junior. But they aren't there, Meg told herself, every time she came. If you believed in anything at all—and certainly, Cornelia was assumed to believe—you knew that. They were no more there than a man is in the clothes which have been sent away for storage.

After the pilgrimage, lunch; in good weather, such as this, on the terrace. Cornelia had been brought up to the heavy midday Sunday dinner, but Andrew Brand hadn't. So they lunched after church, went about their pleasures or duties, took a drive into the country, or, winters, read in the

42

library and had friends in for tea. Dinner was served in the evening.

Always, going home, Meg considered the youngest Andrew, sitting between Ramsay and Clara on the front seat, and thought, as she did every Sunday: It's all right now; he's only a baby. But as he grew into an inquiring and, she prayed, happy little boy, she felt it would be senseless to expose him to that traditional weekly visit in commemoration of physical death, no matter how pleasant the surroundings.

This Sunday, when she appeared in the dining room, her son greeted her with "You're late, Meg." She admitted it cheerfully and said to her mother-in-law, "I'm sorry, Nana. I suppose it's because I turned off the alarm clock."

Cornelia smiled, and answered amiably, "If you want to sleep until noon on your Sundays off, you may, although of course I do like us to attend church as a family." She added, "And anyway you were out late last night."

"Where?" asked Andrew.

Meg said, "I went dancing," and smiled and Andrew said, "Why?" and Clara remarked that he was spilling his milk.

After breakfast they went their various ways, until time to assemble for church. Andrew would be looked after in the church nursery, Cornelia, Meg, and Clara would occupy the Brand pew. This morning at the eleven o'clock service the children's choir was to sing, and as the youngsters rose, Cornelia whispered to Meg, "I can't wait for Andrew to be old enough. . . ."

Of course. Andy had sung in the children's choir, too. Meg, looking at the grave little faces, listening to the young sexless voices, felt her throat tighten. She knew a few of the singing children; they were children or grandchildren of Cornelia's friends; some she had seen at the hospital. A children's choir always moved her. Their solemnity was part joy and the knowledge that when this was over and they had filed out soberly, there would be scrambling and laughter as

43

they took off their robes and prepared to go about their usual mischief-making and impertinences, getting in and out of hot water, some with considerable charm.

Lunch on the terrace was enlivened by Andrew's falling into the pool when Clara had gone into the house for a moment. Morton was in the kitchen and Meg had walked with Cornelia to check on a dogwood which wasn't doing well. At sound of the splash, Cornelia began to run, but Meg ran faster and jumped into the water. It wasn't over her head, but it was over Andrew's. She retrieved her child who, silenced by shock and cold water, was absolutely mute until he was safe and dripping on the terrace, at which point he lifted his voice in plaintive lament. Clara came tearing out of the house and bore him away, no explanations being needed.

Cornelia, white, said, "How many times have we told him . . ." She broke off. She said, "It was our fault of course."

She sat down, trembling. She said, "He might have drowned," and added, "I should fence the pool in——"

Meg said, "He couldn't have drowned, Nana. I was there." It gave her a little silly satisfaction. Cornelia couldn't swim.

Cornelia said, "You might have been at work. . . . Yes," she went on firmly, "I'll have to fence it as it was when it was first built. I was always afraid that Andy would fall in."

"But you told me Andy swam from the time he was three," reminded Meg, and realized that she, too, was dripping. She said, "I'll go change . . . up the back stairs."

Clara came to the door as Meg was getting out of her wet blue frock. "Ruined?" she asked.

"No, it's cotton. . . . Nana thinks the pool should be fenced. She said it used to be."

"When Andy was a baby. But Mr. Brand taught him to swim when he started to walk, and when the pool was enlarged, the fence was taken down."

Meg went into the bathroom to rub herself down, and Clara without a word began putting out dry underthings. She said, "Let me have your wet clothes, Meg."

44

Meg wrapped them in the big towel. She said, "I hadn't expected to swim before dinner." She shivered slightly. "Where's Andrew?"

"Back on the patio with his grandmother. She's reading to him."

No lecture. Meg knew Cornelia could count on Clara for that.

Clara said, the wet bundle under her arm, "I'll just take these out," and added thoughtfully, "Mr. Brand never coddled, you know. He believed a boy should be brought up to take what he called sensible risks."

Dressing, Meg thought: And Andy went on taking them, some not so sensible—riots, revolutions, wars, instant marriage.

RETURNING FROM WORK next day she had no time to stop at Scenic Rest and a car passed her as she started to enter the driveway. It was coming from the Brand house. The driver waved at her and she recognized him and his car a split second afterward—Dr. Thomas Jarvis, a pediatrician. She ground to a halt in front of the house, ran up the steps and inside, calling, "Nana . . . Clara."

Cornelia spoke from the sun porch. She said, "In here. . . . What on earth's the matter?"

"I'm asking you," said Meg. "Is Andrew sick? What was Dr. Jarvis doing here?"

"Sit down," said Cornelia, her strong hand steady on the silver teapot. "No, Andrew isn't ill."

"But what was Jarvis——?"

"I called him," said Cornelia placidly. "This afternoon, after his nap, Andrew seemed a little flushed, even sniffly. I thought it was quite possible he'd caught cold yesterday."

Anger boiled in Meg. She said, shaking her head at the offered cup, "I saw Andrew this morning before I went to work. He was fine."

Cornelia put the rejected cup aside. She said, "I don't like to take chances. Yesterday by one o'clock it was very warm. Andrew had been running about; he was perspiring. And when he fell into the pond, he had a real ducking—right after his lunch."

Meg broke in furiously. She said, "I've had considerable experience with children. I'm a trained nurse, remember? And Clara has had baby-nurse training——"

"You weren't here after Andrew's nap," Cornelia interrupted. "Clara assured me that he was all right. Nevertheless——"

Apparently neither could finish a sentence. "Did she take his temperature?" Meg demanded.

"Well—yes."

"And?"

"It was normal," Cornelia admitted. "However——"

"Clara is perfectly capable of telephoning Dr. Jarvis and of calling me if she believed it necessary. Andrew was in the water a very short time. He was immediately dried and changed."

Cornelia ignored that. She said, "I'd be the one to call Dr. Jarvis." At least those were her words; but her tone sounded as if she'd said, "I give the orders here." She smiled at Meg, and said lightly. "Of course you think I make too much of something possibly trivial. The effective word is 'possibly.' Also, I think you are making too much of my calling Tom Jarvis." She laughed. "He was dying to tell me that I'm a silly old woman, but he didn't."

Meg said, rising, "I was frightened when I saw his car. I'm sorry if I've upset you." She wasn't, and knew it.

"Oh," said Cornelia, "that's all right. You're really the one who's upset. Run along and change, and then do come down for a cup of tea."

Or hemlock thought Meg savagely. She went upstairs. The nursery door was open, and she went in and saw

Andrew dragging the dreadful bunny around, while the little record player was going like crazy.

"Says he's dancing," explained Clara. She took one look at Meg and rose to turn off the player. "That's all for now," she told her charge and at the swift reaction of rebellion added, "Bunny's tuckered out. Sit down and play quietly for a minute before your bath."

"You look as if you were cooking in the shell," she told Meg.

"I am."

"You saw Dr. Jarvis?"

"In his car, on his way out."

"And then," said Clara, "you saw Mrs. Brand?"

Meg nodded. She said, "It infuriated me."

"I suppose so. Let it go, Meg. Andrew was fine. I knew it, naturally. But if she wanted to call the doctor"—Clara shrugged—"what difference does it make? She can afford to call doctors as often as she likes."

After a moment she added, "If there'd been anything wrong, I would have seen to it that the doctor was sent for and you too. As it was, not even a sign of a cold."

"It makes me so *mad*," said Meg. "Honestly, you'd think I didn't know anything—or you either for that matter."

"Well, according to the way she feels about it," said Clara deadpan, "Grandma knows best. Humor her. There's no use getting worked up over something like this. Save your ammunition until a time when you really need it and won't waste it."

Meg laughed. "Wait until you see the whites of her eyes?" she inquired. "Okay. I'm sorry I lost my cool as our younger patients say." On her way to the door, she added, "Sometimes I feel as if I just weren't here. I mean, not really."

Clara said, "You and me both—sometimes." She patted Meg on the shoulder, and then gave her a small shove toward the door. "That uniform's disgraceful," she remarked.

"I know. I've been standing on my head in the files. Also I spilled a little coffee. I hadn't time to change. The boss is in a snit. She's flying south because her mother's ill and I'm in charge for maybe a week, maybe more. God help me."

You can say that again, thought Clara, but not about your boss or the hospital.

Toward the end of the week Meg was in her office which adjoined Mrs. Elgin's larger one. She supposed she could move in to Mrs. Elgin's temporarily, but she had no wish to do so. Her own office suited her well enough. People came and went. She dealt with doctors and surgeons, who cajoled, demanded, or complained; with nurses doing much the same; and with students in tears over bad marks ("Miss Nealy hates me, Mrs. Brand; she just *hates* me"), over trouble at home, over money problems, over reprimands, and heartaches. She dealt also with her own work and flew about on her routine inspections as well as on Mrs. Elgin's. It was a long and overtime day and she was about to call it just that when Charles Scott strolled in with a dark, somewhat shorter man in tow.

Meg stood open-mouthed as Charles said, "No need for introductions, I understand."

"For heaven's sake, Keith Lansing," said Meg helplessly. "What in the world are you doing here?"

He was standing beside her, shaking her hand, retaining it for a moment.

"Snooping," said Charles, sitting sidesaddle on the nearest chair. "God, I'm tired! I explained to Keith that Mrs. Brand wasn't here but you were and he said, 'Not Meg!'—whatever your maiden name was—and raced me to the door."

"We knew each other years ago," Meg said.

"That goes for me and Keith also," said Charles. "In the Navy as it happened. . . . How about supper?"

"Supper!"

"Customary. I can't take you both out; I'm on call. Also, I have a couple of pretty sick patients, as Meg knows, but we can fight our way into the coffee shop, eat sandwiches, and talk for half an hour."

Meg hesitated and Charles remarked casually to Keith Lansing. "She's scared stupid of her mother-in-law."

"I am not!" Meg contradicted, flushing.

"Okay. Prove it. Pick up your phone and call Aunt Cornelia. Tell her you've met an old friend and won't be home for dinner. That's an order."

After a moment, she did so.

"How nice," said Cornelia. "Will you be late, dear?"

"Oh, no, we're just going to have something in the coffee shop."

"I'll tell Andrew you'll look in on him later," said Cornelia.

Meg waved both men out of the office. "I'll meet you," she said, "if there's a table."

She washed up in the bathroom adjoining Mrs. Elgin's offices, powdered her nose, reddened her mouth, and looked at herself critically. Thank heaven, her uniform was clean. She brushed her hair and put her cap back on at a somewhat jaunty angle. She hadn't thought of Keith Lansing in a long time; nor had she heard from him, except during the first few weeks after he had whomped out of her apartment in a name-calling rage. That was the word she'd used to the roommate to whom she was closest. "So, I said, 'No, a thousand times no,' and he just whomped out!"

Of course right after that she had thought of him, wondering if . . . wondering why not? And then she stopped wondering and after a while met Andy. She had spoken of Keith Lansing to him just once, on a sunny Greek island beach.

She thought: Nana will be beside herself trying to figure out how I could possibly meet an old friend in Melton when I've so few new ones, even.

Charles had commandeered a corner table and was looking critically at the sandwich-soup-dessert menu. There were several sandwiches. He shook his head and said to his companion, "Well, you know hospital coffee shops; however, this is better than most. Make a note of it. . . . There's my girl," he added, rising.

"Oh, she is, is she?" said Lansing, getting to his feet.

"Of course. Any pretty girl's my girl. I've cornered the local market," Charles said and then collapsed onto his chair. "I did stand up," he said, "but my feet hurt. You do the honors from now on."

So Dr. Lansing did and Charles remarked, "How elegantly he pulls out a chair. I haven't the strength to do more than rise for a second. I hope you saw my sacrificial gesture, Meg."

She assured him that she had. Then, turning to Keith, she said, "I can't wait to hear why you're in Melton."

Charles waved at a volunteer who came scurrying. "My favorite Hebe," he greeted her tenderly, and she chuckled, being forty-seven. "Bring us three very dry Martinis. Oh, I forgot," he said sighing. "Coffee for three and for me, soup, hot steak sandwich, and the least gooey salad."

Meg said, "Me too," and Keith nodded. With that out of the way, she asked again, "Why are you here?"

"I'm thinking of building a hospital," said Keith, his dark eyes intent on hers, "so I'm traveling around getting some pointers. The Brand was mentioned to me as one of the best of its kind."

"Building a hospital? Not *here*," she said incredulous.

"Nope," said Charles. "Can't you see Aunt Cornelia whetting the dagger—out, damned doctor—forbidding real-estate agents to sell an inch of sacred soil, requiring all contractors to go and contract elsewhere." He turned to Keith. "She's not really my aunt," he explained. "Just Meg's mother-in-law, and this hospital is the work of her mind, money, and persuasion."

"I know about Mrs. Brand," said Keith. "I heard all that before I came here."

"Meg," said Charles, as the coffee appeared, together with the soup, "is her son's widow."

"Oh." His eyes were interested. He had a dark, mobile face revealing, very attractive. "I'm sorry," he said, "I didn't know."

"Save it," Charles advised. "You two can bring each other up to date later. You can drive him to the hotel, Meg," he said generously. "I picked him up and brought him here; he left his car in the hotel parking lot."

Keith said, "That's fine. . . . No, I'm not building anywhere near here; our property is well across the state line. There are several communities there which need a small central hospital. At present there's a good clinic, but when patients need hospitalization, they have to go out of their towns."

"Some even come here," said Charles sadly, "so I've no business to encourage you. However, for the good of humanity, I do. Besides we're usually overcrowded and out-of-state patients add to the load."

"But how . . ." Meg began and flushed, silently cursing her thin skin.

"Like any wise man, or woman for that matter especially doctors, though I'm not talking about hen medics— Keith married into money, as of course, I intend to do," Charles said.

"So you're married?" Meg said to Keith Lansing.

"Yes. While I was in the Navy. Scotty here was my best man, absolutely crocked but conducting himself with great dignity. I thought Frannie would leave me at the altar. She even said, 'If only I'd met him first.' "

"Oh, no she didn't, Lambchop," said Charles, "for if ever I saw a besotted little girl it was your Francesca." He smiled at Meg. "Not that she might not have gotten over Lansing if she'd

51

met me, say a couple of weeks before the crossed swords," he went on modestly, "but, she didn't. Control yourself, Meg; ask what she looks like, where is she from, how many kids— I can tell you that—two at the moment. . . . I have to eat," he added, finishing the soup. "Now we'll talk small voluntary hospitals more or less like this one. You'll have to have Aunt Cornelia meet Keith. She'll love him; they have so much in common."

"Such as what?" demanded Keith.

"Carnivore," said Charles, "charisma, and predatory. Power mad. . . . Here are the sandwiches."

Over sandwiches, they talked hospitals. Keith had looked at a number. He said, "Best so far, this one."

"Some errors even here," said Charles, talking around his sandwich, "I pointed 'em out to you briefly. We'll have another go tomorrow. . . . I can't wait for dessert," he told them.

"Dessert," said Meg astonished, "but we haven't half finished."

"Slow eaters." Charles looked at his watch. "To horse, Doctor Scott," he ordered, addressing himself. "You pick up the check, Lambchop, unless you can persuade Meg to go fifty fifty. . . . Be seeing you."

They watched him make his way out of the coffee shop, stopping to speak to people enroute. Keith said smiling, "Same old Scotty."

"I suppose so," said Meg. "Did you know him well?"

"I thought so. Yes, I'm pretty sure of it. Well enough anyway not to be fooled by his flippancy. But suppose you tell me about yourself. . . ."

It was later than Meg had expected when she drove into the Brand garage. They'd not stayed long at the coffee shop, there were relatives, nurses, doctors crowding into it. After supper she had gone back to the administration offices to talk to the Night Supervisor for whom she had left a report. When she came out, she drove toward the Brand Hotel, but

Keith said, "Don't shed me off so fast—not that I won't see you again; I shall of course. But it's a nice night."

So they drove around for a time and he said, "This is a nice town. Wish I'd seen it first."

"I'm afraid the Meltons and Brands saw it a great many years ago."

"Tell me about your husband."

She told him briefly, and he said, "Well you poor kid," and touched her hand as it lay on the wheel. "What a raw deal."

"Thousands have had and are having raw deals," said Meg. "I have something left—my work and young Andrew."

Morton opened the door for her when she reached the house and Cornelia called from her small study where she was making out checks and writing letters. She asked, as Meg came in, "Did you have a good time?"

"Yes, quite unexpected. . . ."

"Do sit down. Andrew's asleep long ago. . . . Who is your friend, Meg?"

"A Dr. Lansing. I knew him when I was studying for my Master's; he was interning at the time. I haven't seen him since."

"Oh?" said Cornelia, and only her voice raised its eyebrows. "And how did he happen to be in Melton?"

No use not telling; it would be known all over the hospital today, and the town by tomorrow. So Meg said, "He's looking at hospitals. He hopes to build one to serve several small communities, not in this state. He'd heard about ours," —she very nearly said "yours"—"and was, of course, interested."

"How nice," said Cornelia. "Did he like what he saw?"

"Enormously. He'll be back tomorrow."

"Oh?"

Meg said flatly. "He knows Charles Scott; they were in the service together."

"He's staying with the Scotts?"

"No, he's at the hotel."

"It seems to me," said Cornelia, "as long as they are old friends Charles could put him up, unless of course Helen's home."

"Helen?" repeated Meg bewildered.

"Charles's mother," said Cornelia patiently. "I'd like to meet Dr.—what is it?—Lansing. Do you expect to see him again?"

"I doubt it unless he stops by the office. I'm pretty busy with Mrs. Elgin away."

"Well," said Cornelia, "if you do see him, ask him if he has time to call. I'm always interested in people who plan. Is he married?" she asked.

"Oh, yes," said Meg. It amused her to add, "Charles was his best man."

Cornelia let that pass. She said, "If you'd known you were to remain at the hospital for supper, you could have taken a frock and changed."

Meg said, "Well, no one's in the coffee shop but doctors, nurses, aides, technicians, or patients' relatives, and they couldn't care less. I'm sure Keith and Charles didn't. They're used to uniforms."

"Charles was with you?"

"Certainly," said Meg sedately, and left the room.

Five

THERE WAS a muted buzzing about the hospital which Meg recognized—rumors, questions—a new man coming to town? The state inspector? No, it couldn't be the state inspector; practically everyone knew him by sight. People popped in and out of Meg's office and leaving, remarked guilelessly, "Everyone's wondering who the good-looking new doctor is," and several asked, "A friend of yours? I saw him in the coffee shop with you."

Explanations were simple, so Meg made them briefly. The younger nurses, and the students, would she presumed correctly, be extremely disappointed. No, not a new man in this town and for this hospital.

She didn't see Charles Scott except to encounter him in a corridor a couple of times; she did see his father, who came to visit one patient in the surgical wing. Mrs. Green's surgery had been performed by Dr. Meadows, but she wasn't happy unless she saw William Scott daily; so he came regularly, sat by her bed, shooing the private-duty nurse from the room, held her thin old hand and said, "You're going to be all right, Louise."

Charles looked a little, but not much like his father. The older Scott was shorter, heavier, and his thinning hair was gray, and under heavy still-black eyebrows, his eyes were hazel.

Meg stopped by on her routine duties and asked Mrs.

Green, who was on a rather tricky diet, "Was everything satisfactory?" Dr. Scott told her that naturally no patient thought anything satisfactory on any hospital tray, but Mrs. Green would just have to grin and bear it. He followed Meg out of the room and standing by the open door said, "Understand you know Charles's friend, Lansing."

"Yes, long ago," said Meg. She thought: And very far away.

"Smart," said Bill Scott. "He'll go the distance. Can't say I took to him." He looked at her, drawing his shaggy eyebrows together. "Should have had him stay at the house, but with Helen still away . . . Of course Sarah does what she can, but it takes Helen to run a house. . . . You've never met my wife?"

"No," said Meg smiling. "I'd like to."

"So you shall," he said, and turned to go back in the room. He asked, "Everything all right at Cornelia's?"

"Of course," she answered and was somewhat confused when he remarked. "Clara comes up to see Sarah now and again, but she was never a talker."

"Clara?"

"Cousin of Sarah's," he said, went back to his patient and closed the door.

Well for heaven's sake! thought Meg, going on her way, everyone's related to someone around here. She had liked the way Dr. Scott's eyes had lighted up when he spoke his wife's name. There was, she thought, back in the office, something a little odd—perhaps even mysterious, but that sounded so Gothic—about Helen Scott. Nothing you could put your finger on, just Cornelia's occasional cryptic remarks such as the recent one to the effect that Keith Lansing wouldn't be asked to stay with the Scotts if Mrs. Scott *were* home and something she had said about her the night Meg went dancing with Charles, she couldn't recall what it was, and now Dr. Scott saying that the house wasn't guest-worthy when his wife was away. She remembered some of the older nurses saying, "Poor Dr. Scott . . ." All idle speculation. Well, it wasn't her concern in any way.

Someone knocked, and the Chief in Obstetrics came in. She liked him; he had been her doctor when Andrew was born. He was a big, soothing, slow-spoken man, very deft, and comforting; she hadn't had too easy a time, as it happened, a fairly long labor, and she'd remembered her own training and some of the brisk gentlemen who did their efficient jobs and that was that. "Not much humanity left," one of the old-time nurses had said to her in her senior year. "Walk down a ward, look at a chart, sometimes they don't even speak to the patient. Different in my day."

Come to think of it, everyone's day was different.

Dr. Richards discussed his problem with her and then asked about Andrew, "Best-looking boy I ever delivered."

"I bet you say that to all the mamas."

"Certainly. In your case it might even be true." He smiled at her. "You're doing a good job here, Meg," he said.

Praise from Sir Hubert. She went back to the files and Mrs. Elgin's secretary, smiling.

She was almost ready to leave when Keith Lansing came in. "Through for the day?" he asked.

"That's right."

"How about dinner at the hotel?"

Meg shook her head. "Sorry," she said.

"Big date?"

"Hardly. Reacquaintance with my son. He was asleep when I got in yesterday evening and half asleep when I left this morning; and Mrs. Brand is having people in for bridge."

"You used to hate bridge!"

"I still do," said Meg cheerfully..

Lansing helped her on with her coat. He said, "It's hotter than hell outside, you know."

"I know, but I don't bother to change here and it conceals the uniform."

"How about tomorrow night? I was leaving, but I'd stay over. We haven't really talked, you know."

She said, "I'm on duty tomorrow." A spark of mischief ignited, and she added, "Mrs. Brand is anxious to meet you. Could you come for dinner earlier, say, five thirty for a swim and drinks first. I'll see if I can get hold of Charles."

"I'd like to come. Why Charles?"

She didn't answer that. She said, "I'll call you at the hotel tonight. Do you know if Charles is in the hospital?"

"No, he went out on house calls. I still had a little professional snooping to do."

"I'll leave him a note," Meg said.

She wrote it, standing at her desk, went out and left it at the desk to be put in his box. The girl to whom she spoke looked intrigued. By nightfall all her many friends would know that Mrs. Brand was leaving notes for Dr. Charles Scott. Peace, hospital life was wonderful! Any organization that employs a number of people of both sexes is wonderful.

Driving home she put her foot on the brake to avoid a collision with a car which stopped short and without warning right in front of her. Somehow that put both feet, metaphorically, on the ground. She'd never taken it upon herself to ask people to meals before. Cinderella simply did her chores, sat in the ashes, and took orders.

The young Duffs were to be there again that night after dinner, during which Cornelia, Clara, and Meg talked about Andrew, the weather, and the fact that Mrs. Brand felt better now that there was a fence around the pool and a gate made secure. Then the Duffs came for coffee, Clara vanished, and they settled around the bridge table. After a hand or two Meg said brightly, "Nana, I asked Dr. Lansing to come for a swim and dinner tomorrow night. You said you wanted to meet him and he's anxious to meet you. I hope it's all right. I knew you didn't have another engagement, and he's leaving Sunday."

If a slight shock wave passed through Cornelia, she gave no indication of it. She said, "That will be splendid."

"I said I'd phone him at the hotel just in case you did have something on your calendar."

While she was dummy, she telephoned. Dr. Lansing was not in his room, but they paged him in the dining room and bar.

He came finally, and she said, "Keith? Mrs. Brand will expect you at five thirty. I don't know whether Charles can get off or not, I haven't heard."

Lansing said, "How do I get there? Can't rely on Scotty, he might be called out in the middle of a drive. I thank God that my specialty keeps me home nights—or do I?" he added thoughtfully.

She laughed; she knew by now that he was specializing in dermatology.

"Wish you'd stayed and had dinner with me; not a damned thing to do but go to the flicks. I'll try and get hold of Scotty; we might have a drink together when he's through for the night—if he ever is."

When she returned to the bridge table, Cornelia asked casually. "Charles coming too?"

"I don't know. I haven't seen him, but I left him a note. I remembered you said some time ago that it would be nice if he came for a swim."

Which, she thought to herself, you didn't mean.

"Very nice," said Cornelia coolly, looking at her cards; and opened with three spades.

After the Duffs had gone Meg thought: And now I'm supposed to apologize for behaving as if this house belonged to me.

But Cornelia was most affable. She said, "Get yourself to bed, tomorrow's a working day," and added, "I'm curious to meet Dr. Lansing. He's young, of course, Charles's age, and it's unusual to meet a young man with ambition and foresight. I wonder how he intends to raise the money?"

Meg, halfway upstairs said, "According to Charles, Keith married money. He said it in the coffee shop and Keith didn't deny it."

"Dear me, how very like Charles!" Cornelia remarked and then, "Yes, ambition and foresight." She added—a little malice in molasses—"Maybe you should have had the ambition and the foresight——"

"What do you—oh, Keith. No," said Meg. "He had those qualities then too; he wouldn't have permitted himself to become interested in a poor but proud girl trying to make her way in the world."

She went on upstairs, to look in at Andrew and to go to bed wondering what had taken her off course. Charles, of course: Charles on the night of the dance. Charles saying to Keith last night, "She's scared stupid of her mother-in-law." She wondered, before she went to sleep, what Cornelia was thinking. . . .

Cornelia was thinking along a straight, logical line: So that was it. Dr. Lansing couldn't let himself be interested in Meg. But Andy could, she thought, with the proprietary anguish which always stabbed her when she thought, or spoke, of her son. Andy had not been ambitious, except in his profession; nor had he possessed foresight. Having had several narrow escapes from matrimony, his mother had thought perhaps he'd go on escaping, at least until such time as she could select and offer to him the suitable girl with the right background and connections—money wasn't a factor here, although it's always pleasant to have more.

Meg's background and connections were estimable enough; but Meg wasn't someone Cornelia had known since infancy; nor was she someone who would meticulously conform, outwardly at any rate. As, for instance, Irene Martin, who was Cornelia's godchild, and a girl for whom she had once had plans.

On one of his rare visits home, Andy had said to his mother, "Will you stop casting stones?"

60

"Stones?"

"Irene Martin, for one. Handsome, but still a stone; I'll pick my own girls for better or worse; besides she's Scotty's girl."

"Charles? She doesn't give him the time of day when you're around and you know it."

"Proves she's an idiot," Andy Brand had said firmly.

Irene, Cornelia knew, was still abroad. A sudden marriage, a quick divorce, a Paris flat. Her mother often came to tea, saying tearfully, "If only Irene would come home." But Irene was only based at the Paris flat; she was on the Riviera, on an African safari, in Italy, or heaven knew where.

Perhaps she would come home, but not for long, and she'd never marry old dog Tray, who, to anyone's intimate knowledge had not been serious about any young woman since Irene.

In the hospital next morning Charles called Meg at the reception desk. He said, "Thanks for your note. I'll be along, probably a little late. Our mutual friend can get there by himself, his time is his own. Be seeing you. I'm looking forward to an interesting evening."

It was. Meg came home late, but had time to change. Cornelia had Andrew and Clara on the terrace with her. The long glass table had been laid for dinner; the hurricane lamps were judiciously placed and presently, when their guests arrived, there would be swimming and cocktails. Keith Lansing came punctually at five thirty, carrying a flight bag. Meg made the introductions and Cornelia regarded Dr. Lansing as he regarded her. They were, of course, making the usual small talk: "So good of you, Mrs. Brand . . . ," and "I'm delighted to meet a friend of Meg's." That sort of thing. Also, "This your boy, Meg?" and a confrontation between Keith and Andrew, who looked at Dr. Lansing in the honest, if fleeting, appraisal of his age group and then smiled; his smile was Andy's, and Meg never saw it without remembering.

Keith sat down, Andrew climbed into his lap, and Cornelia said, "He rarely takes to strangers so soon."

"I've a boy of my own," said Keith, "older than this one, six to be exact and a four-year-old girl."

Meg asked, "You're prepared to swim, Keith?"

"Of course," at which Andrew said he wanted to swim, but Clara bore him away, remarking that he'd do his swimming in the bathtub.

Meg took her guest into the downstairs guest suite which opened from the terrace and said, "You can change here."

"Quite a house," he said, smiling. "Somehow, you don't fit in."

She thought of her aunt's house in England and how well she fitted there and was homesick.

"Well, you've only seen me in inexpensive restaurants and a crowded little apartment," she reminded him.

"Happy?" he asked as she went to the door and she answered gravely. "No, Keith, not under the circumstances."

"I didn't mean——"

But Meg went upstairs to change again, this time into a bathing suit—brief, becoming, decent—and to pick up her robe and slippers. Looking at herself in the full-length mirror, she reflected dispassionately that marriage and child breeding became her. She was, she thought correctly, more attractive now than when she had thought herself in love with Keith Lansing. He had also altered—not exactly more settled, not exactly more self-assured. Heaven knew he'd been self-assured when she knew him, but—what was the phrase?—toned down, perhaps? He was as good-looking as she recalled, quieter possibly, and with a distinct air of dedication. She laughed aloud, there at the mirror. If she had a fortune, she'd stake it that the dedication wasn't to humanity.

She went to see Andrew, who asked her if the nice man would come to see him. She said, "Perhaps," ruffled his hair and kissed the top of his head as he splashed in the tub surrounded by a floating menagerie. Bunny splashed with him.

"Now and then he insists," said Clara. "At least it gets the little beast clean, and I hang him from his ear on a towel rack."

"It doesn't hurt," said Andrew seriously. "Clara says so."

Meg ran downstairs, slowed to a walk when she reached the bottom. Out on the terrace Doctor Lansing, in bright yellow trunks, a towel draped around his handsome shoulders, was in earnest conversation with his hostess.

"Oh, there you are," said Cornelia unnecessarily as Keith rose and looked at Meg with appreciation.

"Sorry to be so long. I stopped to see Andrew."

Cornelia said, "Dr. Lansing and I have been talking about his project. It interests me very much."

"Mrs. Brand has given me some inestimable pointers," said Keith, "it was fortunate for me that I came to Melton, saw the hospital, met Mrs. Brand, and saw you again," he said, smiling at the younger woman.

Presently they swam. Meg disliked diving and went in from the steps, Keith executed a beautiful dive and came up beside her shaking his thick dark hair back from his forehead. And she asked, "You stay tanned all year?"

"Sun lamp, in moderation." They swam toward the far end of the pool and he said, lowering his voice, "You were always pretty. Now you're sensational. You know I missed you for a long time."

She said courteously, "Thank you. I missed you too for a little while."

Cornelia sat in her high-backed chair. There was a little wind in the trees, the sun was bright on the water of the pool, blue water because the pool lining was blue. She hadn't talked entirely of hospital building costs, and management. She'd said also, "Meg tells me you were friends long ago."

63

"Well, yes." He'd laughed with the sort of frankness that is always suspect. "I was crazy about her, but unfortunately she didn't reciprocate."

"Impractical of her," said Cornelia lightly, "since it's quite evident that you've become a very successful young man."

Keith shrugged. He said, still with that intended-to-disarm candor, "I wouldn't have been, or not as soon anyway, if it hadn't been for Francesca."

"Your wife?"

"Yes."

"Where is she from?"

"Syracuse. She was Francesca Wainwright."

"Oh." Cornelia reflected a moment and then said, "I think I met a Mrs. Wainwright from Syracuse on a world cruise about the time Meg and my son were married in England."

"Fran's mother. She's half Spanish which accounts for her daughter's name. My father-in-law is Horace Wainwright."

"Oh, of course," said Cornelia. She retained a vague impression of Mrs. Wainwright and her husband; pretty woman, somewhat younger than he. She'd met them at the Captain's small cocktail parties and on other occasions; but they were usually surrounded by a younger crowd and went tearing off at the various stops, sight-seeing, amusing themselves. Cornelia preferred small parties, quiet bridge games, and less tourism. She had begged off from sitting at the Captain's table, saying she was honored and so regretted that she wasn't very well and must often dine in her stateroom; or, if in the dining salon, at the early sitting, and could she please have a small table?

It was so arranged. Mrs. Brand was no stranger to ships and faraway places and Captains' tables; besides when Andy's cable reached her, she'd had no wish to be part of a rollicking group.

64

She wasn't sure what Horace Wainwright did. She'd look him up in *Who's Who* later that evening.

Meg and Keith were floating about, he asking a number of questions and she answering them indifferently. Yes, Melton was a pleasant place; yes, she liked the hospital; and of course she liked Charles Scott; he'd been a close friend of Andy's.

Charles arrived after they left the pool. It was warm enough to wrap yourself in a towel, as Keith did, or put on a robe as Meg did, and have before-dinner drinks from the small bar wheeled out by Morton.

With the arrival of drinks, Charles came out to the terrace unannounced and said, "Evening, Aunt Cornelia and Meg. Hi, Lambchop."

"Lambchop!" said Cornelia startled.

"Dr. Lansing," said Charles and sat down. "I'm beat," he said and Meg asked, "How about a swim?"

"Haven't the stamina. Rather have a drink. Long," he instructed Morton, "cold, and very strong. The effects will have worn off, if heaven is kind, by the time I have to rush to someone's bedside. I hope I've time for dinner," he said gloomily and regarded the other three. "Idle rich," he remarked.

"Include me out," Meg told him.

"Okay—if you insist."

"I wish," said Keith, "you'd stop this Lambchop business. Now and again I see someone from the Navy days and Fran blows a gasket. Lambchop!"

"Would it be indiscreet to ask how you earned it?" Meg inquired.

"Very," said Keith.

Charles hooted like an owl. "It's a long story," he said, "and not suitable for the ears of gentlewomen."

"That's what I keep telling Fran," said Keith. "It drives her up the wall; one of the few secrets I've ever kept from her," he added and glanced quickly at Meg.

"One dark day some of your drunken buddies will turn up and brief her," Charles warned him lazily.

"God forbid," said Keith piously.

They drank, they had crackers and cheese and some hot canapés dreamed up by Mrs. Morton and then Cornelia said, "Run off and dress, you two; you're shivering, Meg."

She wasn't, but it was her cue. She rose obediently, guided Keith back to the guest room and herself went up the back stairs. She considered her wardrobe and decided on a plain, rust-colored shift, which was flattering to her hair, skin, and figure. She took from a drawer a sweater which closely matched it. The aquamarines went well with the color.

She wondered what Keith was thinking, but decided she couldn't care less. The word for Keith—she had now found it—was "smug"; not old-smug, young-smug, overlaid with charm. What was the word Charles had used? charisma. She found herself more interested in wondering what Charles and Cornelia might be talking about.

They were talking about Dr. Lansing. "I like him," said Cornelia. "I like a young man with ambition."

"Unlike me and Andy?" Charles suggested lazily, squinting against the declining sun, enjoying the aftereffects of Morton's well-fortified Scotch, water, and ice.

She said sharply, "Andy was ambitious, Charles."

"Oh, in his work, sure. But the kind of drive Lambchop radiates wasn't in Andy."

"That ridiculous nickname."

"Not really," Charles said and added, "It seems almost unreal to be here again."

"There was no reason why you shouldn't have come long before and often," said Cornelia smoothly, "but it took Meg to persuade you."

"She'd persuade anyone," said Charles, "to almost anything."

"Including Dr. Lansing," said Cornelia. "Well, of course they're old friends. . . . Has your mother returned?"

"Back next week or the week after."

"She's been away quite a while."

"All those babies," said Charles, a careless gesture suggesting two or three hundred. "Sal has her hands full."

Cornelia tried again. "How is your father?" she wanted to know.

"The terrible-tempered Doctor Scott? Oh, he's doing as well as can be expected. Maybe when Mom gets home he'll behave. He's quite forgotten my expensive medical education as far as he's concerned. I'm just a second-year student."

Cornelia said after a minute. "I do wish he'd come to see me."

"He won't," said Charles amiably.

"So silly," said Cornelia as if he hadn't spoken, "that idiotic quarrel, and each of us too proud"—she smiled—"or stubborn to admit himself in the wrong."

"I haven't the foggiest notion what it was all about," said Charles, lying in his handsome teeth, "or who was in the wrong, as you put it."

"We both were. I miss him," said Cornelia.

"I'm sure you do," said Charles without expression and she looked at him quickly. But his face was a closed book. After a while she said, "Do talk to me about the hospital. Honestly, Meg hardly talks of it at all and I'd like some——"

"Inside information outside the board room? Well, usually I'm too damned busy——"

"Must you swear?"

"I didn't really and you never used to mind it, or are you just remembering I was in your Sunday-school class?"

Cornelia laughed. She said, "Well, continue."

"——too busy to know what's going on around me outside of me, myself, my patients, the consultants, and all that. Now and then I hear something—locker-room stuff—a funny episode or two which I can repeat without turning stool pigeon, or is it informer?"

Cornelia was laughing when Keith emerged from the house, followed a moment later by Meg.

Charles whistled and Keith gave her a long thoughtful look. Charles said, "One look is as good as two whistles—anyway married men can't whistle, or shouldn't."

Morton announced dinner.

Six

D INNER was excellent and, as dusk deepened, the hurricane lamps burned in their glass shelter with an almost unwavering golden light. Halfway through dinner, there was a crash, a child screaming, and the sound of Clara's running steps on the stairs. Meg was on her feet and running, too, with Charles right behind her.

Cornelia, after a convulsive start, sat quite still and then motioned Morton. "Dr. Lansing's wine glass," she said, and then as Morton hesitated, spoke again. "The doctor's glass."

Keith was on his feet; he said, "Perhaps there's something I can do?"

Cornelia gestured him back to his chair. She said, "Meg's there, and Clara, and"—a little reluctantly—"Charles. Someone will come presently and tell us what happened."

They came, in a small procession, Andrew sobbing, in Clara's arms and Meg said, "It's all right, Nana. He got to the stairs and fell. He's not hurt, except in his pride—he rolled down, I think."

She was white, but she smiled and Clara, more agitated than Cornelia had seen her in a long time, said, "He was in bed, Mrs. Brand. When I went to get him a drink of water, he climbed out——"

Cornelia held out her arms, Clara relinquished the child and Cornelia said, "You're all right, Andrew."

Meg said, "Charles, will you come upstairs and look him

over?" but Andrew, his flushed face wet with angry tears, pointed at Keith and demanded, "Him . . ."

Keith, looking pleased, started to rise and Charles said, "A dermatologist—how much have you forgotten?" He scooped Andrew from his grandmother's grasp, paying no attention to redoubled howls and marched off with Clara and Meg in his wake.

"Well," said Keith, "I'm flattered of course, but Scotty has an imperious way with him."

Cornelia said, "Andrew's never attempted anything like it before. I'll have a gate put up first thing tomorrow. He fell in the pool recently, which is the reason for the rather disturbing fence. . . . Do eat, Dr. Lansing, everything will be stone cold."

Meg and Charles returned and Charles said cheerfully, "No damage; a small bump on the head and, tomorrow, bruises on his bottom. He was scared mostly—but he fell completely relaxed, as a child often does—or a drunk."

Cornelia said, "I'll have Tom Jarvis see him tomorrow."

"By all means," said Charles politely, and Meg opened her mouth to say, "But that won't be necessary, Nana," caught Charles's swift, warning look and said nothing. Keith was a little amused. What, he wondered, was going on here? Of course any idiot could see the surface—but, underneath . . .?

In the middle of delayed dessert the telephone rang and Charles said, "Oh, my prophetic soul!" and left the table before Morton reached the terrace.

"Only under the most unusual circumstances," Keith said, "am I ever called and deprived of dinner."

Charles joined them. "Back to the treadmill, salt mines or, if you prefer, Brand Memorial," he said. "Thank you, Aunt Cornelia, for having me. You leaving tomorrow, Lambchop?"

Lambchop was.

"Drop by the hospital if you get a chance." He waved at Meg, "See you around," he told her.

Coffee in the living room, and general conversation during which Meg twice excused herself to see if Andrew was asleep. While she was out of the room, Keith was aware that he was being gently pumped: about his practice, his wife, and his old friendship with Mrs. Brand, daughter-in-law. This entertained him and he employed his specialized candor where he thought it called for, not otherwise.

His hostess said, "It must be a little dull—I can't even offer you television."

"Why not?" asked Keith. "You should get good reception; it's fine in the hotel which, by the way, I've found very comfortable."

"I don't like the medium," Cornelia said. "Now and then I'm compelled to watch in my friends' homes. Much ado about nothing—motion—noise"—she shrugged—"and what appears to be psychedelic backgrounds. I'd rather Andrew were not exposed to it."

"He will be," said Keith, "as soon as he's old enough to visit his contemporaries; he'll come home, demanding a set of his own."

"We'll see," said Cornelia.

When Meg returned from her second absence, Keith rose and said he must go, much as he disliked to. "I want to call Fran," he explained, "and tell her I'll get an early start in the morning."

After the usual courteous exchanges, Cornelia began, mechanically, "Morton will see you—no," she went on, changing her mind, "Meg will walk to the car with you. And I do hope I—we see you again, Dr. Lansing."

He almost found himself saying, "Likewise, I'm sure," and then he was outside with Meg. He said, "You didn't have to convoy me, Meg—but that sounded like something starting with, 'Now hear this.'"

"It was," said Meg, laughing.

"We've had practically no time together."

"Coffee shop," she reminded him, "a drive around town, a swim today and dinner."

"I meant, alone."

She said, "So I assumed."

"I'll be back," he told her. "It isn't very far, you know."

"I hope you'll bring Mrs. Lansing with you," she said.

"Not for a while. She's pregnant and her mother is always nervous about her when she achieves an interesting condition."

"Oh? Has she reason to be nervous?"

"None whatsoever. Frannie's a strong, healthy young woman," said Mrs. Lansing's husband, "but I humor my mother-in-law." He added thoughtfully. "And so do you."

He was driving an expensive convertible, and the top was down. He leaned from his car, kissed Meg's cheek, said, "So much for old time's sake," and drove away.

Meg went back to the house, half annoyed, half amused, and still shaken by Andrew's tumble. She found Cornelia in her office gravely studying the pages of *Who's Who*. "This thing weighs a ton," she complained. "Well, did you see him off?"

"Yes. . . . Whatever are you doing with that?"

"Looking up the Wainwrights. Mrs. Lansing's mother was half Spanish, titles too," she said vaguely, "and Mr. Wainwright is president of a very large corporation, and on the boards of half a dozen more. I'd say your old—what *does* one say nowadays, follower? suitor?—boyfriend had done very well for himself."

Meg said, "Well he wasn't really . . ." stopped, shrugged mentally, and added, "I'm glad for him, and it was a pleasant evening except for Andrew's accident."

"I telephoned Tom Jarvis," said Cornelia. "He didn't think it was necessary to come tonight and upset the child again; he said Charles was perfectly competent. He'll be over in the morning, unless of course something untoward develops and I call again."

"Nothing will develop," said Meg shortly and then, "Good night, Nana." She left Cornelia putting *Who's Who* back on the shelf and went upstairs. Clara heard her, and emerged from Andrew's room. "He's still asleep," she said, "and none the worse for the acrobatics. Mrs. Brand will have Ramsay go to the attic and get the gate we had when Andy was little and put it across the stairs. I feel bad about it. He might have been really hurt, but I never thought—he's never done it before, but he took quite a fancy to Charles's friend—perhaps he was looking for him."

"It wasn't your fault," Meg assured her, and put her arm around Clara's shoulders.

"Mrs. Brand will think so. We knew he was agile as a monkey, but he's never gone crib-climbing before. I'll have to grow eyes in the back of my head, as I did when Andy was a baby. But that," said Clara, "was a long time ago."

Meg was having lunch in the coffee shop when Charles barrelled in and made for the table at which she was sitting alone. He sat down, said, "Coffee," to a volunteer, grinned, and added, "Please," and then turned to Meg.

"How are things?"

"Under control."

"I suppose Tom will have seen the kid by now, or did Aunt Cornelia call him last night?"

"She called him; he told her you were competent and that unless something unforeseen developed he'd be out first thing this morning."

"Oh, I'm competent all right," said Charles. "I recognize concussion, skull fracture, broken bones. . . . Lansing stay late?"

"No. He had to telephone his wife and get an early start this morning. Did he stop by to see you?"

"No. He'll be home in time for church. Always correct Lambchop—well, nearly always."

Meg reflected that Cornelia would probably attend church

alone today, leaving Clara and Andrew, and would thereafter make her solitary pilgrimage. She had no doubt that during prayers Cornelia would gently reprimand God for permitting Andrew to fall downstairs.

Charles asked, "How well did you know Keith Lansing, actually?"

"Well enough," said Meg. "I fancied myself in love with him." She smiled brilliantly. "A carbon copy," she added, "of the real thing. Anyway, it was of no significance to either of us. . . . What was he like in the Navy?"

"Efficient and devoted to the ladies, to use a general term. But cautious, until he met Francesca."

"Is she attractive?"

"Physically?" asked Charles. "Oh, yes, very."

"Did you know she was pregnant now."

"Yep, Lambchop told me. I don't know how she feels about it, but my deduction is that he's delighted to keep her that way, within reason. She's something of a mama's girl. Her mother, incidentally, is as attractive as Francesca, and more volatile. The Lansings live almost next door to the Wainwrights, in a house which was a wedding present. I imagine that his in-laws think highly of your old friend."

"That makes three."

"Who's the third, you or Francesca?"

Meg laughed. "Three children."

"Oh, well," said Charles, "they can afford half a dozen and I'd make an educated guess that the Wainwrights would be pleased. How Francesca feels about the population explosion I'd have no idea. For the brief time I knew her I considered her like the description of the French in the old geography books—you know, fond of light wines and dancing?"

He finished his coffee, said, "Let me know how Andrew is. It cut me to the quick to have him prefer Lambchop to me. Andrew's father was also given to snap judgments; but at

74

least one of them," he said, smiling, "was A-okay. . . . We'll have a date soon, God and Aunt Cornelia willing."

In due time Mrs. Elgin came back to the Brand and, after reading reports and making tours of inspection, rewarded Meg with the Navy, "Well done." Meg had been glad of the boss's return. She was tired and summer was still blazing hot, although in August the nights cooled off and spoke of autumn, not too remote. Life went on, the mixture as before, outwardly, at least, calm enough. Andrew barred from pool and stairs found divers ways to elude Clara. He was growing almost under his womenfolks' eyes. He was also talking a great deal. Charles suggested when she spoke of it, "Andy was a talker, too."

Keith Lansing did not return to Melton; he wrote after his visit to Mrs. Brand, thanking her for her hospitality, adding, "Give my love to Meg and Andrew, and my best to Scotty when you see him." Cornelia gave the note to Meg without comment.

Whether or not she liked it, Cornelia was seeing Charles Scott. He dropped by now and then; he telephoned. Meg had dinner with him once at the hotel; and then Helen Scott came home from California.

She drifted into the hospital, light as a blowing leaf and came into Meg's office, as if timidly. She was a tall, over-slender woman with a worn and lovely face. There was a pewter streak in her brown hair; and her eyes were dark gray as were her son's. She said, "Mrs. Brand? I'm Charles's mother, Helen Scott."

Meg rose, smiling. She said, "How nice of you to come see me."

"I wanted to meet you." When Helen Scott smiled, she looked ten years younger. She said, "Always face up to your rival."

"Rival?"

"Bill and Charles are devoted to you," said Helen. A

75

shadow crossed her face, the tired lines came back. She said, "I was terribly fond of Andy, Mrs. Brand."

"Try Meg."

"Thank you, I shall. I wondered, if you'd come to dinner with us one night when you are free and I can pin Charles down?"

Meg said she'd like that, and presently Helen Scott drifted out again and Meg sat down and looked thoughtfully at the calendar on the desk. Charles's mother was not at all as she had imagined her. Somehow she had thought of her as round, rosy, full of bounce, although now that she thought about it, Charles hadn't really given her that impression.

Going home she thought about the older woman's eyes— gray, like her son's, and deep set, but lacking the laughter lines etched around Charles's eyes; hers were somber eyes, almost tragic, and when she'd sat down by the desk, like a frightened child's.

That night, after Clara had gone upstairs, Meg told Cornelia over coffee, about her unexpected caller.

"She must think Charles is serious about you," said Cornelia placidly. "Is he, by the way?"

"Not to my knowledge." What was serious? A kiss, or two, or even three? A casual word, a warning against involvement?

"Are you going?"

"I'd like to," Meg said warily.

"You'll get a good dinner. Sarah, who runs the house with the help of a daughter, is a good plain cook. You won't, however, get anything to drink."

Meg said startled, "What's unusual about that?" But thought of Charles, demanding a strong Scotch one night on the terrace.

"Nothing, I daresay. However Helen Scott has been an alcoholic for years. I believe her illness has now been, as they say, arrested."

76

"Oh!" said Meg. "Poor woman."

"Years ago," said Cornelia, "it was very difficult, for her husband and son and her friends. I was once quite close to her. We all did our best. Now and then she consented to, I believe the euphemism was 'go away for a rest.' She'd come back looking quite splendid, except for her eyes. Did you by chance notice her eyes?"

"Yes," said Meg shortly.

"We would all be so happy for her, so careful of her," Cornelia went on, "and then it would happen again. And as long as we're on the subject, I may as well tell you that my quarrel with Bill Scott was over his wife—why, is of no consequence. She heard about it—how, is also of no consequence—and would have nothing to do with me thereafter. She didn't, however, try to stop Charles from being with Andy. Eventually, of course, they went their separate ways for quite ordinary reasons—schools, universities, war."

She rose, saying she had letters to write and added, "I'll be interested to know what kind of an evening you spend."

The engagement was made by Charles, coming into the office, saying, "Mom wants to know how about Wednesday. I'm off that night presumably. Preston is covering for me. I'll pick you up, round six thirty."

Meg had time to go home that evening, take a quick dip, and change before he came.

Cornelia appeared to see them off and to ask, "Would you like a drink, Charles? I've persuaded Clara to a sherry."

He said, "Well, just a short vodka perhaps," and looked at Meg. "How about you?"

She said, "No thanks, it's too hot."

It was a sultry, thundery sort of evening, heat lightning ripping the sky, but as yet, no rain. Charles was asking Clara how he could get himself into Andrew's good graces and Clara was saying it shouldn't be hard.

"But I'm not Dr. Lansing."

"He's forgotten him," said Clara.

On the way to the Scott house, across town and up on a hill, Charles said, "I daresay, knowing Aunt Cornelia, she's briefed you about my mother."

Meg was not to be drawn. So he said crossly, "She needn't have bothered; Mom will tell you herself. It used to embarrass the hell out of Pop and me too but"—he shrugged—"we're used to it. It's one of the ways in which she punishes herself, I think."

Meg said, "I'm sorry, Charles," and then, embarrassed for him, added, "but there's no need for her to say anything to me, Charles. I'm a stranger."

"It's in strangers that she usually confides," he said. "However, she's as aware as I am that her one-time bosom pal will have issued a bulletin. Also, she knows I'm in love with you."

"Which is more than I do," Meg told him with considerable spirit.

Dr. Scott used a short effective word, then said, "I'm sorry. But don't try to put me on. You know it, I know it, my parents know it, and good old Aunt Cornelia suspects it. So everyone, including me, is trying to figure out what we're going to do about it."

To her own astonishment Meg began to laugh. She said, "Even conceding you're telling the truth—which I doubt—two questions arise."

"Such as?"

"One, what makes you think I'm in love with you?"

He said gloomily, "I don't think it, but given time and opportunity I think you could be. What's the other question?"

"Merely, why should we do anything about it?"

"You're not that naïve," said Charles.

"I hardly know you," she began and stopped abruptly.

"You thought I was going to say, 'And you hardly knew Andy, either'? I wasn't. Actually, you know me a little better than you did him."

"That's perfectly absurd!"

"Is it?" he asked gently. "I don't think so. You fell in love with Andy immediately. You hadn't had time to know him, then or even afterwards. I'm willing to give you time."

"Well, thanks."

"You're welcome. Of course you understand that if you do come around to my way of thinking and feeling, The Dowager would fight it tooth and nail and by every available means."

She said indignantly, "I can make up my own mind."

"Can you? There's Andrew to think about. If you hadn't considered him all this time, you'd have taken him under your arm and fled long since."

"But there's nothing she can *do*."

"I wouldn't be too sure."

They were in the town now and presently turning away from it. He said, "Don't be fooled by my mother. She has guts; if she hadn't, she wouldn't have asked you here. But she hasn't seen me, so to speak, in this pitiable condition for a long time, not in fact since Irene Martin. Did dear Nana ever tell you about Irene and me?"

"No—who is she?"

"Melton girl with looks and money. I fell in love with her; she preferred Andy and Cornelia approved. Andy wasn't interested, or at any rate not seriously. Story of my life in the appropriate nutshell."

Meg had never heard of Irene Martin. She asked, "What happened to her?"

"Marriage and divorce. She lives in Europe. That was one time when our benevolent spider couldn't catch the fly."

Meg said, "Andy didn't tell me about her."

"There was nothing to tell. He was charming to her, after she grew up, but when he found I was howling at the moon, he stopped being charming to Miss Martin. I daresay if he'd been in love with her, he'd have swept me out of his way in no time flat, old friend or not. But he wasn't—in love with her, I mean."

"Poor Andy," said Meg, thinking of him with love, amusement, and to her amazement, detachment.

"Why? He had everything going for him, always, until that damned bomb."

"I didn't mean that," said Meg. "I meant—I suppose Irene whatever her name is now, has blamed her marriage and divorce on him."

"She wouldn't be the first to do just that."

"I suppose not."

"Let's get back to us."

"I didn't change the topic, Charles."

"We can pull it off——"

"What an extraordinary thing to say."

"Not really," he said. "If you can love me, really love me——"

"Are you proposing to me?"

"In a manner of speaking. I can support you and Andrew. I like that little cuss even if he can't stand me. I suppose this is where I say I'd be a good father to him—Okay, so I've said it—and also to my own children, eventually."

After a moment, Meg said painfully, "I like you so much and I'm a little in love with you, I think. No one has ever attracted me as much since—but——"

"You want the time I offered you?"

"That's right."

He turned into a driveway. He said, "Okay. So I won't announce it yet. Satisfied?"

He stopped the car, and as he helped her from it, he kissed her, quickly but thoroughly. "Into the house," he ordered. "Fast."

Seven

~

M EG WENT UP the wide steps, across the roofed porch
and waited. She found she was shaking slightly;
whether because of the evening before her or
Charles's brief but demanding kiss, or possibly both. He came
up the steps two at a time and said, "Don't let the fact that the
house is falling down distress you," and opened the door.

This was an elderly house, and big; the entrance hall
was wide, and contained considerable furniture; a chest of
drawers, a table, chairs beside it, lamps, and a bowl of
flowers.

"Hi," said Charles. "Anyone home?"

His mother came out from the living room. She said,
"We didn't hear you come, we were watching the news. How
nice to have you here, Meg."

She was wearing a floor-length frock, leaf brown, traced
with yellow. Meg took the offered hand, long, narrow and
cold and thought: She's scared too. A surge of compassion
flooded her for this seemingly fragile, somewhat withdrawn
woman, who in her own way, had fought, lost, and won her
private battles; in between them, the armistices.

Still holding Meg's hand, Helen Scott went into the
living room and Charles's father turned off the TV and rose,
nursing his pipe. He said, "It's about time. Glad to have you
aboard, Meg."

The room was comfortably shabby. Here and there the

soft yellow of the painted walls was scarred, as was the furniture, also comfortable and shabby. But someone had polished it to a high sheen.

Helen drew Meg over to a small sofa, indicated an ash tray on the table beside her and opened a silver box of cigarettes. Meg shook her head. "I don't smoke," she said, smiling.

"You're lucky," Helen told her. "It's a filthy, dangerous, and expensive habit. I smoke too much."

"You can say that again," said her husband. He shook his head. "There's nothing I can do," he told Meg. "She listens, but doesn't obey."

Helen said, "Charles, perhaps Meg would like tomato juice or cranberry?" She looked at Meg. "There's really no reason why I can't serve alcohol to my family and guests, but Bill won't let me."

Meg said, "I don't drink much, Mrs. Scott."

"That's right," said Charles. "Very inexpensive girl to take out, which is one of the numerous reasons why I like her."

Helen said, "Cranberry?" and when Meg nodded, said, "Suppose you do the honors, Charles?"

She takes it for granted, Meg thought, that someone— for someone, read Cornelia—had explained the situation, but if Helen minded, she didn't show it.

As Cornelia had predicted, dinner was good. Sarah's daughter served and toward dessert, which was apple pie, Sarah bounced into the room, a round cheerful little person, highly informal. She said she was dying to meet Andy's wife.

Helen performed the unnecessary introductions and Sarah's bright, sharp blue eyes looked Meg over; then nodding as if satisfied, she said, "One of my cousin's girls, Edna Morris, works at the Brand; she graduated from there; she says, you're just fine." Reaching the kitchen door, she looked over her shoulder and spoke to Meg again. She said, "You tell that Clara to come see me."

Shortly after they'd had coffee in the living room—and it *was* a lived-in room—Helen excused herself. She said, smiling faintly, "I usually go up to bed about this time, and read—I'm sorry."

Meg rose. She said, "I'm sorry too."

"I tire easily," Helen told her. "They give me shots and keep me on high protein diet, but I still tire."

It showed in her delicately made-up face, in the lines, and under the dusting of powder and perhaps rouge, she was white.

They all went with her to the hall. William Scott went upstairs with her and when Charles and Meg returned to the living room, she was aware that unobtrusive, quiet Helen Scott left a lasting impression behind her.

Breaking a short silence, during which Charles smoked and walked about as if she were not there, picking up a newspaper, glancing at a book, Meg said, "Your mother isn't strong, Charles."

"Physically, no. Pop worries about her twenty-four hours a day, whether she's here or away. Me, too."

He sat down, halfway across the room. "Do you like her?" he asked abruptly.

"Very much," she began and he said, "Don't be sorry for her, Meg."

Her traitorous color rose. She said, "I'm not."

"Yes, you are. Everyone's sorry for her; it's one of the things she's had to fight. The so-called understanding. It's widespread in Melton. People have acted for years as if they were tiptoeing around a funeral home. It's the last thing she wants or needs and she doesn't want that type of understanding either. What she needs is love."

"Which I'm certain she has."

"Of course, my father, my sister and her family, me and Sarah. Sarah would cut her throat tomorrow for Mom; and, also from a few friends." He started to say something further, but apparently decided against it. Then after a moment he went on, "A woman who needs love and attention, a woman inclined toward loneliness—well, she has a rough time as a doctor's wife. With my father, much as he loved her, the profession had to come first. Maybe with me, too. I don't know," he added smiling, "never having been married. But I aim to find out. This is in the nature of a warning, Buster."

Dr. Scott came back into the room. He said, "She's tucked up with half a dozen books. All of us make frequent trips to the book shop's lending library. Sarah, her daughter, sometimes even I go or Charles. We can't keep her supplied. She reads late, Meg."

Charles said somberly, "It's an escape."

"Oh, your mother knows that." He turned to Meg. "About this time Charles and I have a drink together. If he's called out I wait till he returns. How about you, Meg?"

"After that good dinner!"

"A liqueur then? Settle for a tot of brandy?"

She said she would and when he had left the room, looked at Charles, "I don't understand wholly."

He said, "Mom knows the ritual. It doesn't upset her; she's never present."

Dr. Scott returned with a tray; highballs for himself and his son, a little glass of brandy for their guest. He said, tinkling the ice in his glass, "You've made a hit, young lady. Runs in the family."

Charles took Meg home early. "Tomorrow you've a living to earn; me too," he reminded her.

At the door Meg said to William Scott, "It was such a lovely evening."

"*Agape*," said Charles, "Greek for love feast."

"Don't show off," said his father testily. "I've read a book or two myself, and no doubt Meg has also."

Charles ignored that. He said, "And so different from dinner at Aunt Cornelia's which was pure hubris."

"Oh, shut up," said his father, "and take your girl home." He added, "Charles has recently discovered Greece."

She thought of this as she got into the car and found herself saying, "I did, too."

"You did what too?" asked Charles. "Here I am ready to tell you the uninteresting story of my personal life, and you aren't even listening."

"I was thinking about what your father said—that you'd recently discovered Greece."

"So you said you had too—with Andy, of course."

"Just for a little while." She was silent a moment, seeing the sand and the water, a vivid but miniature picture, gradually receding. Then she said forlornly, "But I'm beginning to forget."

He felt the sharp excitement of triumph and carefully kept it from his voice, saying easily, "I don't think so, Meg."

"Andy, too," she said quietly. "I don't even see him clearly any more—photographs are static—except in flashes, and occasional dreams. It's strange, and frightening."

He said, "Not so strange, Meg. You'll always remember because it's all part of you, woven into the pattern—just as your childhood is, and your growing up."

She thought about that for a moment. Then she said, "Mrs. Brand—Nana—continuously remembers, aloud, as if challenging me to forget for one instant. You do, too."

"I thought you'd want me to talk about Andy."

"I do," she said, "in a way; but in a way, not. I never knew the child Nana knew, or the boy who was your best friend."

"I'm sorry, Meg."

"About what, that I didn't know him?"

"Yes, I suppose so, but mostly because you're learning a tough lesson. The moment does last, honey; it's not preserved as a glacier preserves, as a little insect remains in amber, a seahorse captured in lucite, a shell, or a fossil trapped in a cabinet. The moment goes on, or it dims and wanes; it doesn't mark time, it isn't static."

"But Nana——"

"You're not Nana by a good many years." He took her hand, put it on the wheel and laid his own over it. "How long can you endure living in a temple dedicated to the dead?" he asked.

"At first," she said, "I didn't realize it; I was numb I suppose; and also ill. And then Andrew was born, I was well again and no longer numb. I hurt, all over. Now, mostly I think about getting away. But as you yourself said, Andrew has to be my first concern."

He said, "You'll get away, Meg, if I have to bake the loaf of bread with the file in it, myself. I daresay Aunt Cornelia has already asked you, however delicately, what, if any, are my intentions."

"You've been eavesdropping," she said, laughing.

"I don't have to, I had a lot of time, years ago in which to study Andy's mother and try to figure her out. Incidentally, she'll put you through more than one interrogation."

"What shall I tell her?" she asked, half seriously.

"That my intentions are honorable, and you're considering the matter."

"Which brings us to your parents."

"They like you," he said gravely, "and they love me. Even if they didn't like you, Meg, that would be the same."

"Although they aren't on good terms with Nana?"

"That's right, and has absolutely nothing to do with you."

They had reached the Brand driveway. He said, "Take it easy, don't let her put you down. You're a big girl now."

"If Andy had lived," she asked, "what would it have been like for me—and her?"

"Armed truce on her part. Believe it or not, I'm certain she was a little alarmed by Andy; he had a good deal of his father in him, as well as his mother's—shall we call it determination? But Andy would never have brought you here for any length of time. Probably you would have lived all over the world and come to Melton only occasionally, seen Aunt Cornelia in London, Paris—or wherever Andy was for the time. He probably would have asked her to fly in for a week or so. It would have been very different, Meg. For your sake, I wish to God it could have been that way."

She said suddenly, "Andrew is to grow up in the Melton-Brand tradition, schools, university, everything."

"He won't be his father," Charles said gently, "or his grandfather, or any of his ancestors. Oh, here and there a gene of course, but he'll be himself, an individual."

"I don't know," said Meg unhappily. "He's a baby now and malleable."

"If the genes are Brand," said Charles, "as well as Melton, the stubborn streak for instance, the emphasis on the personal, undominated life—Andy had that emphasis, and his father, too—Nana will not be successful. And we'll see to it," he added, "that the exposure isn't too long."

He stopped the car, took her in his arms, and kissed her. He said, "I'll take you in and we'll face the Wagnerian music together."

"Why Wagnerian?"

"Oh, you know, the distant thunder, the threat, the intimidation of the affronted gods."

This time, Cornelia was waiting up. She was playing records, not Wagnerian, and reading. She said, "Well, come in, you two. I didn't expect you so early."

"I'm a working man," said Charles, "and Meg's a slave to Mrs. Elgin. Good evening, Aunt Cornelia, how are you?"

"Very well, thank you—and your father and mother?"

"In great form. Pop rages around, declaring he's well enough to return to his father's horse-and-buggy house calls. Mom's blooming," he added unabashed. "California and the strenuous life did her good."

He smiled at Meg, who said, "I had such a good time," and Charles answered, "Fine, we'll do it often. Don't bother to come to the door, I know my way out."

When he'd gone, Cornelia said, "Morton has a slight cold. I sent him off to bed. . . . Oh, I should have offered Charles a drink; very remiss of me."

Meg said cheerfully, "He and his father had one before Charles brought me home."

"Really?" said Cornelia. "And you and Helen?"

"I had a little brandy; Mrs. Scott had gone to bed."

"Oh? What do you think of her?"

"I like her very much; she a charming woman."

"Well, poor creature," said Cornelia.

Meg said sharply, "Why do you say that? I'm not in the least sorry for her."

"You don't know her," said Cornelia tolerantly. "Most people who do, like her, but are also sorry for her."

"They needn't be," said Meg with spirit; "she can fight her own battles."

"I see she's found a champion."

Meg said, "She doesn't need one. Good night, Nana. I'll stop in and speak to Clara, I have a message for her."

"From whom?"

But she didn't answer, she was running up the stairs and when she had inquired for Andrew and taken a look at him, she drew Clara into the hall and said, "Sarah what's her name——"

"Jones," said Clara straight-faced.

"Well, anyway, she told me to tell you to come see her."

"I'll go when I can manage. I know she's dying to see Andrew, but, for that, she'll have to come see me."

"Why? I can take Andrew to see her with you, Clara, when I have some free time."

"Off limits," said Clara. She stopped, they could hear the record player, but Clara said, "Come into my room for a minute."

Once there, she shut the door. She said, "The Brands—and that includes Andrew—don't go calling on the Scotts."

"But Mrs. Scott is interested in Andrew," Meg said. "She asked me a dozen questions about him at dinner, and she spoke of Andy as if she'd been very fond of him."

"She was."

"It's all so stupid," said Meg, "just because Nana and Dr. Scott quarrelled——"

"Mrs. Brand told you that?"

"Yes, she said it was over Mrs. Scott. I can understand it, in a way; if she wanted to help her—oh, Clara for heaven's sake, I know all about that—and Dr. Scott was angry. I suppose he thought her interfering."

"Well, it wasn't quite as you think," said Clara. "Go to bed, Meg." She looked at her a moment and then said slowly, "I believe you're in love with Charles Scott."

"I don't know whether I am or not," said Meg crossly. Then she put her arm around Clara, "I suppose everyone—you, Nana, even Morton and Mrs. Morton—would hate me if I decided that I am."

"I wouldn't," said Clara, "nor would the Mortons." She kissed Meg's cheek. Any demonstration of affection from Clara was rare. Even Andrew knew that. She said, "I hope you are. He's a fine man, Meg, and he's had a lot on his plate."

Meg went to bed and lay wakeful for a time, trying to sort out her own emotions, thinking of Helen Scott as well as Charles; thinking too of Andy, uneasily, as if apologetically, wretched in a way and, in a way, happy. No, she would not apologize to Andy even in her mind. But the stupid words were there, the guilt feeling: "I didn't mean to fall in love." How much sense did that make? Few people ever mean to. And the other inevitable words, "I do love you, I'll always love you, but you aren't *here*."

No, not in her mind, not even in her heart, could she explain, justify herself, ask his pardon. He'd know, she thought, if there were any way of knowing. He might even say, as he'd said on several occasions, "Oh, stop bugging yourself, darling; everything's going to be all right. You'll see, that's my good girl."

She couldn't remember why he'd said that to her; perhaps because she'd fretted about his mother. She recalled asking once, "But won't she dislike me?" and he'd said, "Who could?"

Remembering brought him closer, and she had one of her sudden flashes of visual memory; his expression, his eyes, laughing at her; it was almost as if she could hear his voice, that of the sometimes impatient, occasionally demanding but understanding man she'd known.

She wrenched her thoughts back to Clara's remark that the Brands didn't call on the Scotts. Meg could have argued, "But the Scotts—at least one of them—called on the Brands." Clara would have said merely, "Well, Mrs. Brand can't help that, can she?"

Of course not. Charles had come to see her, Meg, and Cornelia could scarcely throw him out bodily. Morton was hardly up to that. And it would have distressed him to close the door saying, "Neither Mrs. Brand is at home." Besides Cornelia, always averse to scenes, would probably have deduced that in such a case Meg would open the door saying, "This Mrs. Brand is."

However, Cornelia had known that Saturday evening Charles would be crossing the Brand moat and scaling the walls; she could have spoken her piece well before his arrival.

Meg thought sleepily, and with gratitude of Helen and William Scott. However they felt, whatever had caused the breach, they had received Andy's widow, and no questions asked.

Friday, when Meg came back from the hospital, Cornelia said, "Two letters for you—one from your aunt." She gave Meg her mail and did not so much as raise the eyebrow, although she had probably seen the return address on the other.

Meg opened that one first. "It's from Keith Lansing," she said evenly. "He'll be coming through here next week on his way upstate and says he'll remain overnight if you and I will have dinner with him—yours to select where."

Cornelia said, "How amiable of him. Thank him for me, but say no. You know I dislike going to restaurants, Meg. . . . Or wait; I've a better idea. Say I'd like to take him to the country club; he might enjoy it. I fancy he's a rather country-club type."

She did not suggest that Charles be included, or that Meg alone might have accepted Keith's invitation.

As Meg was about to go upstairs, Cornelia told her idly, "Charles stopped by this morning; he was coming from a house call. . . . Perhaps he told you?"

"I didn't see him today."

"He claimed he wanted to see Andrew"—Cornelia smiled slightly—"as Andrew had been his emergency patient—not that he didn't trust Tom Jarvis."

"And did he see him?"

"Naturally. Andrew seemed delighted."

DURING THE DAYS before Keith registered at the hotel, Meg saw very little of Charles Scott—only in corridors, the lounge, a nurse's station, or the coffee shop. At the shop, scalding himself with coffee, he said, "As usual I'll stick you with the check, Meg."

She said, "Keith's coming through here day after to-morrow."

"Why?"

"He said he was going upstate."

"Probably to take a look at the Cornish Memorial. I spoke about it to him."

"He asked Nana and me to dinner——"

"Ah, so?" Charles grinned. "And?"

"She refused; says she doesn't like restaurants, but then she decided she'd take him to the country club."

"She didn't ask me," said Charles sadly.

"No." Meg scowled slightly. "Something rather odd is going on, I think."

"Operation Throw Meg to the Wolves?" Charles asked cheerfully.

"Possibly," she admitted.

"More power to her. All she needs is an ember breath of scandal and you, my darling goose, are cooked."

"She didn't suggest that I go with him alone——" Meg began.

"She wouldn't. Her ways are devious. She chooses to chaperone you heavily. Would you have gone with him, alone?"

"I don't think so."

"Chicken."

"First I'm a goose, then I'm chicken," she said indignantly. "No, I just didn't want to, and I don't want to go to the Club, either."

"I'll try to be there," said Charles, "and bring a gorgeous girl, which will mystify Nana and I hope annoy you. 'Bye, see you around as often as possible."

Dr. Lansing was made welcome at the Brand Hotel, as welcome as if he were a constant guest. He had a productive technique in hotels, restaurants, motels, or resorts; he tipped well, he was pleasant (but not familiar), and he complained only when even a waiter, chambermaid, or the management was aware he had sufficient grounds.

Once settled, he telephoned Cornelia. If the dragon is necessary, placate the dragon. This was a game; there'd be a time when the dragon would retreat to her cave. He'd played the game before. There were certain fixed rules, and some you made up as you went along. He had played games (never recklessly) before his marriage; and also (cautiously) since. But never until this had he played with such a strong opponent.

Cornelia was, she said, happy to know of his arrival. She asked, "You came by car?"

He had and she went on, "There's no need to use it tonight. We'll pick you up a little after seven. I regret to say that as the evening wears on the Country Club cuisine becomes leftovers."

After that he showered, changed, tossing his tie in the wastebasket—Frannie had deplorable taste in ties—called Charles at the hospital, and left a message for him.

Shortly before Ramsay arrived with Cornelia and Meg, Charles telephoned. He said, "Welcome back."

"Thanks."

"Going to Cornish Memorial?"

"That's right."

"We're better," Charles said, "but they do have an innovation or two, also pretty nurses, the majority of them. I noticed that fleetingly when I went up for a state conference last spring. Sorry I'm not free for dinner."

"I'm not either. Our friend Mrs. Brand is taking me to the Country Club."

"Wonderful," said Charles. "You'll love it. . . . Which Mrs. Brand?"

"Both, although it was the elder who issued the invitation."

"Don't work on her, Lambchop."

"Which one?"

"As you just said, both, but in this instance I was thinking of my quasi-aunt Cornelia. I'd hate to have you siphon off any funds needed by our home-town project."

"Oh," said Keith carelessly, "I don't need funds—at least not now."

"Lucky bastard."

"Thanks, pal," said his old friend. "Mama never told me."

They were both laughing as they hung up.

93

Eight

ORNELIA made her accustomed entrance, serene, smiling, gracious, but those in the dining room who knew her—and few did not—experienced the familiar awareness of muted fanfares and invisible couriers dispensing largesse, and almost all were curious about the identity of the young man in the white dinner jacket.

Cornelia wore mauve, Meg, pale green, and Keith looked at them appreciatively as they were seated at what was definitely the Brand table.

"Best-looking girls in the room," he said and Cornelia and Meg spoke simultaneously; Cornelia murmured, "How nice," and Meg said, "To coin a cliché."

"I wasn't coining clichés or being nice," he protested, "just honest." He smiled at Cornelia. "Meg," he remarked, "has developed a sharp tongue."

"Just a part of growing up," Meg explained.

He remarked thoughtfully, "She was really naïve, innocent—and kind when I first knew her."

"Oh, but she still is," said Cornelia brightly.

"I hope not, Nana," Meg said, looking back at the girl Keith had known—stupid, trusting, half-enchanted. She felt a stab of compassion for her; she regretted her as one regrets the death of someone almost forgotten. "You both make me sound all sweetness and light."

Now Cornelia and Keith spoke together. Each said, "I didn't mean that!"

During dinner Meg and Keith danced. Cornelia had

urged it. "Do dance," she said, "the service here is incredible; you'll have plenty of time between courses."

Keith asked at once, "Would you dance with me, Mrs. Brand?"

Cornelia shook her head, "I haven't danced in years."

"Good old girl," said Keith, out on the dance floor; "she lets you off the leash now and then."

"She wouldn't thank you for the adjectives. And any leash is of my own making."

"I surmise because of Andrew?"

She did not answer and then he asked, holding her closer, but not too obviously, "How is he by the way?"

"He's fine, you asked in the car."

"But I didn't ask you, I asked his Nana. . . . I don't have to be at Cornish until tomorrow afternoon. What are my chances of seeing you alone?"

"None. I'm working tomorrow."

"Somehow, somewhere, I'm going to manage to see you, Meg."

She said, "Perhaps now's as good a time as any to assure you I'm not interested."

"You were, once."

"Oh, yes," said Meg indifferently. She smiled, "But that was in another country and besides 'the wench is dead.' "

"You sound like Scotty. Greatest guy for quotations I ever knew, drunk or sober. Frannie was dazzled. I remember one thing he said, when someone came up to wish me happiness. Scotty advised solemnly, "Call no man happy till he dies."

"Herodotus, paraphrased."

"I see he's been teaching you."

Meg said serenely, "I read a book now and then."

She had read a great deal, in the days after Keith and before Andy: nonselective, catholic, indigestible. After Andy's death she could not read fiction for a long time. When she read at all, it was biography, history, easy-to-assimilate philosophy, and the medical journals.

"Speaking of you know whom," said Keith, as they returned to their table.

Charles and a girl were sitting with Cornelia. Keith whistled and Meg smiled. She said, "She's exceptionally pretty."

"You know her?"

"Of course; she does private duty at the hospital."

She knew something else; she knew that little Sophie Keble was engaged to a Melton boy now in Vietnam. He'd been reported missing a while back and it was Charles who had seen Sophie through her desolation. Meg hoped she had also helped. Later, when it had been established that Roger was a prisoner, Charles and Meg went on helping, for the desolation now included fear.

Charles rose, the blonde girl smiled at Meg, and Dr. Lansing was presented. Charles said, "Come on, Sophie, I've just time for a dance and a drink."

Sophie spoke to Meg. "I've been on night duty until a couple of days ago. Meg, when you have time, will you come to the house some evening—for supper maybe? I'm going back on nights next week."

When they left, Cornelia explained Sophie to Keith. "She lives with her parents," she told him. "Her fiancé's a prisoner of war."

"Vietnam? That's rough."

"She's a nice child," said Cornelia. "I must admit I was a little astonished to see her here."

Meg said, "Charles is her doctor. One of his prescriptions is that she get away from the house, from the hospital, when she can."

"Does he always take his patients' prescriptions?" asked Keith.

Cornelia said mildly, "Charles has never ceased to be one

96

of the most popular men in town."

On the way back to the hotel, Cornelia asked about Francesca Lansing. "How is she?" she inquired.

"Frannie's fine," said her husband, "coddled of course and, therefore, happy."

Meg asked, not really caring, "When's the baby due?"

"October."

"She'll have her hands full," Cornelia predicted.

"Oh, not really. She's engaged the same nurse—perhaps you remember her, Meg—Jessie Thorpe, who was with her during her other deliveries and who came home with her each time. When she leaves, Mrs. Tompkins takes over. She's been with us ever since Wainwright, the elder of our present two, was born. Trained, reliable, efficient, rather like your Clara, Mrs. Brand."

"No one," said Cornelia firmly, "is like Clara. She's in a class by herself."

Ramsay stopped at the hotel and Keith got out. He said, "Thank you for an exceptional evening. But next time I come this way, I insist upon being host."

"You plan another trip?" asked Cornelia.

"Possibly." He looked at Meg. "I'd like Frannie to meet you," he told them both. "Perhaps I'll bring her before winter sets in."

As they neared the Brand house Cornelia said thoughtfully, "He doesn't give up, does he?"

Meg asked cautiously, "Give up what?"

Cornelia laughed. "Perhaps you were naïve once, but surely it's obvious he didn't return to Melton to see me, Meg."

Meg said, "He didn't come to see me, Nana, but to look at the hospital under Charles's guidance."

Cornelia shrugged. "That was the first time. . . . Cornish Memorial is not extraordinary," she added. "He could find a dozen comparable hospitals in his own state—and probably has. No, your Dr. Lansing has a long memory."

"He's also a happily married man."

Cornelia said carefully, "Perhaps. But I gather from the little he's said that his wife, apart from being secure financially—she's the Wainwrights' only child you know—is spoiled, which, I assume, means demanding."

"That has nothing to do with me, Nana. I couldn't care less about Keith Lansing or his wife."

"What's the song about old soldiers? They never die but merely fade away; something like that; the same often applies to old suitors."

"Which he wasn't."

"I have a different impression. It would be unfortunate, however, to become involved with this attractive—and, I'm certain, astute—young man. I don't imagine his Francesca would tolerate it."

"I've no intention . . ." Meg began furiously. Then, as the car stopped, she asked, "If you feel this way, however erroneously, why did you ask him tonight?"

"Common courtesy," Cornelia said serenely as Morton opened the door and they went into the house. "Besides, I thought it would amuse you."

"It didn't," said Meg.

In her own room, after her usual whispered conference with Clara, she thought of Charles: Operation Throwing Meg to the Wolves? But why? Because she couldn't marry Lansing . . . because, as Charles had suggested, a scandal, however slight, would increase Cornelia's claim to Andrew.

Before she slept she had decided that, if this were true, her mother-in-law—the prototype of conformity and rectitude, a model of virtue, the faithful widow and inconsolable mother—was probably the most amoral woman she'd ever met.

It would be infinitely more to Cornelia's purpose if Meg involved herself with Keith Lansing than with Charles Scott, because Charles was free to marry.

She thought: And so am I. No matter what the feud, quarrel—call it anything—between the Scott family and Cornelia, there was no way in which Cornelia could prevent Meg's remarriage. Cornelia would have to concede that Andrew's exposure to an ex-alcoholic step-grandmother would hardly be grounds for demanding his custody.

For the first time since her arrival in Melton, Meg found herself wondering if her situation would have been different had Andy's father lived. She thought so, yet she knew so little of him; Andy had said very little about his father; nor had Cornelia about her late husband; only Clara had spoken of him, in reference to his son. Meg knew he had been a handsome man—his portrait, his photographs, showed that—quiet, scholarly but, according to Clara, a believer in taking risks.

Cornelia must have loved him (as she had loved their son) passionately; at least the outward trappings seemed to indicate it: the house which was a shrine; the living memorials, the hospital, the generous gifts to library and church—and the weekly meditations in the cemetery. Cornelia had built a wall around herself; you could go so far and no further; you could look over the wall, but not through it. She sat behind it, dedicated to her sorrow. Everyone in Melton realized and respected it. Andy must have known it, but Meg could not recall his ever speaking of it to her, which was odd; it would have been natural to make the usual comment, "My mother never got over my father's death," although Andy would have phrased it differently.

She thought: I must talk to Charles.

They made the engagement standing at the desk on the male medical floor.

"You free Wednesday night, Charles?"

"Unless there's an emergency. Why?"

"Would you take me to dinner?"

"Alone?"

"Of course."

"No of course about it. Sure. I suggest Bassett's. Ever been there?"

"No. Where is it?"

"A little way out on the road to Cornish. Plain, good, secluded; a pub type, run actually by a homesick Englishman. Pints. Darts. That sort of thing. Could even make you home-sick. I suggest you meet me there. I have to have a get-away car," he explained sadly, "because I'll leave my number where it will do other people the most good. Make it eight o'clock. And don't bother to wear sequins." He added that he hoped when they met she'd still be in one piece and walked away as the loud speaker was querulously calling his name.

Meg went on her accustomed rounds and returned to her office conscious of more excitement than trepidation, and also of the fact that the charge nurse at the desk and those who went by on their usual errands had taken the normal amount of interest in Meg's bright head close to the younger Dr. Scott's.

She didn't inform Cornelia of her plans until Tuesday at dinner, when Cornelia said that the Procters had tele-phoned and would be at dinner on the following night, "and a little bridge if you're not too tired," to which Meg responded that she was sorry, but she had another engagement. "I'm going to have dinner with Charles. He's usually more or less free Wednesdays."

Cornelia's becomingly reddened mouth tightened. She said, "But I told you I'd asked the Procters and that they'd let me know. It was a question whether or not their daughter and her family were coming before the weekend."

"I'm sorry, Nana," said Meg. "I'd forgotten," which was entirely true.

"You could rearrange——"

"No," said Meg, "we have something to discuss."

Cornelia waited until Morton had left the room. She then commented, "It must be important."

Meg smiled. "More important, to me, at least," she agreed, "than dinner and contract with the Procters."

The rest of the meal was conducted in silence except for a meaningless exchange of views on the weather, and Cornelia's remarks about a recent hospital board meeting. Always conceal your emotions from servants was Cornelia's theory; no matter how devoted they are, no matter how much you do for them, all hired help talk. It constitutes drama in their lives. Cornelia did not believe Clara talked—much; she was certain that Ramsay chattered and that the Mortons enlivened their sober lives with discussions of what went on in the household. She did not blame them; she simply guarded herself against what she would call incidents.

On Wednesday when Meg came in from work, Cornelia said she thought Andrew looked a little flushed, but conceded he had been playing hard all day and had not slept much during his nap time.

"Has Clara taken his temperature?"

Cornelia said, "I suggested it after he left me. She hasn't been downstairs since."

"Then," said Meg cheerfully, "he's all right."

On her way from the room, "When will Charles pick you up?" asked Cornelia. "Perhaps in time to have a drink with us?"

Meg said, in mid-flight, "He's not coming here Nana; I'm meeting him."

She went on upstairs and regarded her healthy and amiable son, who said, "What's new?"

Meg looked at Clara. She asked, "Where did he get that from?"

"Charles, I think," said Clara, "the time he stopped by— now and then he comes out with it. Little pitchers."

"Little parrots," said Meg. "His grandmother thought he seemed overexcited this evening."

"His temperature is normal," said Clara with a slight emphasis on the possessive pronoun, and added carelessly, "I understand you're going out tonight."

"That's right," said Meg. She picked Andrew up, disreputable bunny and all, and hugged him. She said, "Wish me luck."

"What's luck?" demanded Andrew, interested.

"It's something I hope you'll always have, and all good, darling."

She came downstairs about a quarter past seven. The Procters were there; a pleasant, friendly contemporary of Cornelia's, and Morton was taking orders. Cornelia asked, "Have you time for a drink, dear?" and Meg shook her head. She said, "You forget, I'm driving." To Cornelia's guests she said she was sorry that she had a previous engagement.

"Have fun," said Mr. Procter and looked at her with appreciation. Mrs. Procter said, "Really, Meg, you look about eighteen. It's hard to believe you're little Andrew's mother."

"Isn't it?" agreed Cornelia smoothly and added, "Where can I reach you, if necessary?"

"At a place called Bassett's on the Cornish Road. I've never been there."

Cornelia's eyebrow rose slightly. She said, "Neither have I. I've heard about it, of course."

Meg asked with interest, "Don't tell me it's a den of iniquity."

"Hardly," said Mr. Procter; "quiet, respectable, and serves the best steak hereabouts. Edna and I go there occasionally. It reminds her of home."

Mrs. Procter was London born. She said, "Bassett is a dear old thing. Looks rather like the breed of the same name, very mournful. We chatter away when I go there. I've often wondered why he stays on here."

"Well, we don't know why he came in the first place," her husband reminded her, "right after the Second World War. Remember, Edna? Then he married the Nostrand girl. Maybe she doesn't want to go to England and maybe he's realized that sometimes it doesn't pay to be nostalgic—going back always puts things on a different light."

"Not for me," said his wife stoutly.

"That's something else again," he said. "You go back for visits, not to remain. Remember us to Bassett, Meg, and tell him we'll drop in some night soon."

"Hasn't he any other name?"

"Probably Henry," said Mrs. Procter. "He was in service before the war, and his father and grandfather before him. Big house—up from boot boy to butler, you might say. But the war changed all that."

"And," said her husband, "the Victoria Cross."

Meg said good night, assured Cornelia that she wouldn't be late and went out to where she had parked her car. She looked at the directions Charles had left in her office: Straight out to the main highway, left turn half a mile on, and then the stretch of the Cornish Road. Bassett's on the right, some miles along, an old farm house.

Once out of Melton, and then off the traveled roads, the way she took was twisting and dark and she drove slowly, aware of a curious anticipatory happiness, not as much from knowing where she was going, as from the fact that she was on her way alone, and briefly, free. When she took her car out—Cornelia's car she reminded herself sharply—it was to go to work and to return. She had not visited anyone of whom Cornelia approved—until of course, she'd gone to the Scotts'.

She did not even worry over what she was going to say, although she had last night. Nervously wakeful, she had thought: Suppose I say, "What are we going to do about us?"

Now she was conscious only of the dark drive and the wind, a little crisp, and the smooth motion of the car and of

103

the fact that she was not only driving steadily toward someone and a future but away from someone and the past. But not from Andy. Charles would understand that.

As she turned into the parking lot, she saw Charles's car. She closed and locked her own and went up wide wooden steps and into a small square hall occupied by Victorian furniture and a coat rack. She took off her top coat. Beneath it she was wearing a pullover, a tweed skirt, and a cardigan. No sequins.

On her right, the bar; on her left, the small dining room; she hesitated looking into the bar. There were people around it and at tables. It didn't look like an English pub, but it felt like one. Then she saw Charles, who rose from a corner table and came toward her.

"I thought you'd chickened out."

"There you go again."

"Or were lost."

"I made only one wrong turn, quickly rectified," she said, "but I drove slowly."

"You look as if you'd enjoyed it." He had taken her hand, and retained it. He said, "I sat here worried, nursing a pint of bitter. What will you have?"

"The same."

She looked around. There was the dart board. The place smelled of good beer and ale and of polishing wax. She said, "I like it here."

"So do I. That's Bassett behind the bar. His wife takes over in the dining room and a waitress will come in presently."

Bassett came over, smiling sadly. Long, thin, droopy. She thought of Edna Procter's description and smiled. Charles made the introductions—so it was Milton, not as Mrs. Procter had suggested, Henry Bassett.

"Old friend of mine," said Charles.

Bassett agreed. "You can say that again, the doctor saw

my Missus through her pneumonia last winter. . . . What's your pleasure, Miss?" he asked Meg.

Charles said, "Same as mine, my second, her first."

"Righto," said Bassett, and left them.

He had a faint patina of pure cockney overlaid by a part-time American accent.

"Did you know he had the Victoria Cross?" Meg asked.

"Oh, yes. Who told you?"

"The Procters."

"Edna and Harry? When?"

"Tonight; they're dining with Nana."

"Oh, sure. Old cronies in a sense—Harry Procter's the president of the bank. How did you get away?"

"I just said I was going."

"And where?"

"Of course, in case of any emergency—at least that was the idea."

Bassett arrived with the libations. Meg spoke to him of England, and his hound's eyes brightened. It seemed he knew the village where her aunt lived; he'd been in service not far from there, he told her, with old Lord Evanston. "He's gone," said Bassett sorrowfully, "during the war, that was. Later Her Ladyship"—he didn't quite drop his h's, or add them either—"went off to Australia, where her daughter was. The estate's a show place—downstairs, that is for the trippers; upstairs, it's been put into flats. Seems a pity."

A waitress came in and Meg said, "I saw Mr. and Mrs. Procter tonight—they asked to be remembered, Mr. Bassett."

"Just Bassett. . . . I've missed them lately. Mrs. Procter and me, we have long talks when the place isn't crowded." He added, "When she goes home, she always brings something back for me—I prize the Coronation mug most."

"Have you ever been back?" Meg asked.

He shook his head. "I'd like to, but the Little Woman, she doesn't fancy traveling. Boston's as far as she goes, gets seasick she does, and is afraid of planes, and you can't drive over water, though I daresay they'll be doing that too someday the way things are going."

He went off, and they consulted the menu. Charles said, "Steak, beef, chops, steak and kidney pie—you name it, they have it. But seafood's for Fridays only."

They settled for steak and kidney pie, and salad.

"Tell me about Bassett's Little Woman."

"Certainly, although you surely didn't come here in order to learn that she's a local girl, inherited this house, the land with it and some money when her widowed father died. Bassett had something put aside too. I've no idea how he drifted this way. Seems to me I've heard it was because he got friendly with a Yank somewhere. But after the war jobs were hard to come by and butlers were a shilling a dozen. Bassett's Little Woman was a good cook. That's the story except that Bassett's a citizen and proud of it. Serves on several committees."

"In Cornish?"

"This is still Melton, Luv. Aunt Cornelia knows our Bassett."

"She said she'd never been here."

"Just because she knows him, why should she see? I believe they've had a run in or two; something to do with the library. Bassett can be very John Bull at times. I must present you to the Little Woman before we leave."

They talked over the excellent dinner and when coffee was replenished and the crackers and sharp cheese before them, Charles said, "You didn't ask me to take you to dinner— and don't deny that you asked me—to talk about Andrew, the hospital, Sophie Keble's difficulties, Melton, and the Bassetts."

"No."

"Then, what? Lie down on the couch, darling, and tell good old Dr. Freud your dreams."

She said, smiling, "All about you, Doctor."

"Splendid," said Charles, his eyes bright. "And so?"

"How serious have you been these past weeks?"

"It cost you something to ask that," he said, "but not as much as if you didn't know the answer."

"Then," she said, looking directly at him, "what are we going to do about it?"

Nine

W HEN YOU'RE EXCITED," Charles remarked irrelevantly, "your eyes blaze like the sea with the sun
on it; and sometimes they darken; sea-colored eyes
and hair like the sunset."

She laughed despite herself. "Aren't you ever really
serious?" she asked.

"Frequently, usually when I'm clowning. I love you,
Meg."

"You haven't answered my question."

"Oh, but I have. If you want it spelled out—just what
was it you asked me?"

"What are we going to do?"

"About us? It's simple enough; we get married and live
happily forever after, barring spells of bad temper on my
part, nagging on yours, interminable discussions, arguments,
quarrels, and reconciliations. Nothing is static. No marriage
runs on an even keel. Forty years of smooth sailing would be
the Sargasso Sea."

She said, "But it isn't simple. There's Andrew and Nana."

"Andrew will be fine. We'll give him a gang of kids to
play with and dominate—redheads with gray eyes, for instance, and dark ones with blue. He'll like that, I think. As
for his Nana the hell with her; it will be of her own
making. . . . You're scared?"

"I'm scared."

"How often must I tell you you're a big girl now?"

"You warned me we shouldn't become involved."

"So I did. It's just as well I paid no attention to myself."

Meg took a deep breath. She said, "Once you told me you didn't know what the quarrel was between your parents and Nana. I didn't believe you. I think you lied to me. Did you?"

"Yes."

"Can you tell me now?"

"No, darling," he said gravely. "There was a time when I didn't know. Andy and I used to speculate about it, a couple of troubled kids. Later, I knew."

"Did Andy?"

"I doubt it; if so, it didn't come from me. And I won't tell you, Meg, because it's something—the only thing, I think—that I can't share with you. It had nothing to do with me, or with Andy—that is, not directly. Can you let it go at that?"

"If you say so," she told him after a moment.

He put his hand over hers on the table. He said, "The next move is yours. It won't be easy."

"Telling Nana, you mean?"

"That's right."

"What will she do?"

"What can she do, except throw you out—and watch us take you in?"

"But she'll try to keep Andrew."

"She can't. You're his mother. The most she could do is disinherit him."

He was watching her closely, saw the little wave of shock pass through her and her eyes darken, and asked, "Does that bother you very much?"

"I suppose, in a way—but it's not the money; it's that it wouldn't be fair to Andrew or his father."

"Cornelia would argue that you aren't being fair to Andy.

She has made a fetish of fidelity," he added and the sharp edge of bitterness in his tone astonished and disturbed her.

She said hesitantly, "In a way, you can't blame her."

"Maybe *you* can't. I can." He looked years older and unyielding. He said presently, "I can look after Andrew; he'll have everything a kid needs; we'll see to that. What does a child need most, Meg? Love, respect, a strong body, an active mind. The body and mind he has already; all they require is care, and freedom to grow. Love he's had since he was born—and I don't mean his grandmother's obsession."

"Obsession? . . . Yes, I suppose you're right."

"Andrew's an individual in miniature—he isn't merely a product of the Brand-Melton genes and yours. He's himself. I've said this before."

"I know that," she said steadily. "And perhaps you won't understand this; I don't like my mother-in-law. I admire her, for certain qualities, and I'm sorry for her, because of her husband, because of Andy; and now to take Andrew from her—"

"Thereby depriving her of her favorite toy, a future docile puppet? But the strings are bound to break. They have broken before—Andy broke his, and neither he nor his father could be manipulated for long. Did you know our kids will have a dash of Irish blood?"

"No," she said, diverted, "though I should have. Where does it come from?"

"My mother's family, far back—a restless Irishman from the north. Quakers they were, believe it or not. He came to this country. . . . Why are you laughing? Is it at the thought of producing a small Sean or Kathleen?"

"No." She was quiet. His hand, still on hers, was strong; there was warmth in it, vitality and reassurance.

"What are you thinking, then?"

She said honestly, "I was thinking of Andy."

His hand stayed where it was, steady and firm.

"I expect you to think of Andy, often—and especially, now."

She said looking at him with candor, "I told you once, didn't I, that he seems far away? But he sometimes comes closer, as now. I'll always love him, Charles. But not as I love you. If this troubles you, it's not too late——"

He said gently, "That was a dream, Meg, a short and lovely dream. You should cherish it. It isn't, of course, our dream—that will take a little time."

He thought: All right, Andy, she won't wholly forget; I won't. And I'm not afraid. I'm glad for you both that you had the little time together. But the future will be my time, and I believe a long one.

The telephone on the bar rang. Bassett answered and came quietly to their table. He said, "It's for you, Doctor."

"Oh, damn and blast you, Bassett," said Charles. He took his hand from Meg's and went to the bar as Bassett murmured comfortably, "Yes, sir."

To Meg, he said, "That's the greatest bloke"—he swallowed and corrected himself—"gentleman."

"Yes. Did you know my husband, Andrew Brand?" she asked.

"Off and on, Mrs. Brand, he wasn't in Melton often after I came here. I was sorry when I heard. I wrote his mother; she sent me an answer. She's a lady," he said; "not that we always see eye to eye."

He was somewhat off balance apparently as his accent was more marked.

Charles threaded his way back. He pulled some bills from his pocket and put them on the table. He said, "If I owe you, or you me, we'll straighten it out another time. Take care of Trix, will you, Bassett?" Trix being their waitress. "Come on, Meg," he said. "It's an emergency."

They collected her coat and walked out to the parking lot. "Sophie," he said, "poor kid. They got her to the hospital and pumped her out; she's asking for me. Where the hell did I go wrong? Seems she was looking at some pictures—in a paper or magazine——"

She said, "Charles, she'll be all right. It's not hearing, the inability to get through, the uncertainty—and reading about the starving and the executions."

"For God's sake," he said. "I know all that! But I should have been able to prevent this."

In the parking lot, people were getting out of cars or into them. Charles paid no attention; they might as well have been alone in the world. He took her in his arms roughly. He said, "I'm going to drive, fast. You take it easy. I'll call you before I go on home—which may be early morning—I don't know, Meg. Be careful."

"You, too." She put her head against his shoulder briefly, he released her and ran to his car. She stood there listening to the angry squeal of tires and watched him barrel out of the parking lot. Then she went to her own car and a man, getting into his, remarked, "Your friend drives like a bat out of hell."

She said, "He's a doctor; he has to get back to the hospital."

"If he doesn't look out, he'll be in it," said the man gloomily.

Driving away, she thought: But he'll get there all in one piece, no matter how troubled he is. She thought: A shoulder to lean on. It seemed to her now that this was exactly what she'd always wanted, and what her aunt had supplied when she was small. Then she grew older and was on her own. Keith? She smiled in the darkness, thinking of his inadequacy. "Andy?" she asked herself. She hadn't had time to find out. He'd made their plans, of course; he led, she followed; but there had never been a crisis, or a confrontation with something terrifying or unhappy. Nothing had touched them until their separation—not loss or disease, not poverty or unhappiness. She would never know. It hadn't come into the dream.

With Charles she'd know, whatever happened. She was as sure of that, without proof, as she was that she was young, alive, in love, and loving.

The Procters were just leaving when she went into the house. Morton was fussing with wraps, Cornelia was saying good-by and then to Meg, "Hello."

"Hi," said Meg to no one in particular and everyone in general and Edna Procter thought: She's more than pretty, or am I just imagining it? She looks as if she'd just come into a fortune.

The Procters said pleasant things about the evening and that they hoped Meg would be there next time and Cornelia added, "Well, even if we didn't have our bridge, it was great fun." She looked at Meg and said, "I haven't played poker in years, but Harry persuaded me."

"I'm sorry I broke up the game," said Meg mechanically, but Harry Procter laughed. He said, "I don't believe Cornelia hasn't played in years. She's nearly as good as Andrew was—I remember those days, Cornelia."

"For a banker," said Cornelia austerely, "you take grave risks."

"Don't we all? But don't fret, I can always rob the bank," and went out with his wife.

"I thought you wouldn't get back in time to see them again," Cornelia remarked.

"I'm afraid I'd have been later," Meg said, "but Charles had an emergency and had to rush back to town."

"I see. I don't have to ask you if you had a good time."

"Does it show? Bassett's is wonderful and so is Bassett."

"He's made something of himself," said Cornelia. "I see him now and again. He's on the Library Committee, and Edna works with me at the Guild. Bassett and I have had our differences of opinion." She stopped, and smiled. Then she said, "A butler—imagine. . . ." She looked around to be sure Morton had retreated, saw that he had, and added, "It's a curious thing, a democratic society. Sit down a moment, Meg, and tell me about Bassett's."

Meg said, "I have to go to work tomorrow, and I'm sleepy. . . . Oh, if the telephone rings in the middle of the night or early morning it will be for me. Charles said he'd call before he went on home no matter what the time, so perhaps you'd better turn off your bedside phone."

There was a device which did this if Cornelia on some rare occasion wished to sleep late. "I'll hear it and take it in the hall," Meg went on.

Telephones all over: upstairs hall for Clara's use, kitchen, garage, living room, Cornelia's office, and bedroom.

"Well, I'm glad you warned me," said Cornelia. "I must say Charles isn't very considerate. Couldn't it wait until you get to the hospital?"

By tomorrow quite a few people would know about Sophie and someone was bound to tell Cornelia. "I'd rather not wait to hear. It's Sophie Keble, Nana; she was brought in very ill," Meg said.

She was on the stairs now not waiting to hear the inevitable questions: What happened? An accident? Pneumonia? And from the top of the stairs she said, "Good night, Nana."

Upstairs she knocked softly on Clara's door and Clara opened it, her gray hair in a net, her gray robe clutched about her. She looked at Meg and shut the door. The bedside light was on, Clara had been reading. All she said was, "Congratulations."

Meg hugged her. She said, "I'm so happy, Clara."

"Me, too." Clara hesitated. "Have you told Mrs. Brand?" she asked.

"Not yet. I'm scared, of course, but it isn't that. I'd like to remember tonight—without fireworks. Tomorrow, when I get back from work, I'll face it."

"It won't be music," Clara predicted.

Meg kissed her. She said, "Well, once more wish me

luck—and if you hear the phone ring between now and dawn, don't worry. I've briefed Nana; she'll turn hers off, and I'll take the call up here."

"Merciful heavens," said Clara. "What's happened?"

"It's Sophie." Meg explained briefly and added, "I haven't reported the details to Nana. She'll learn soon enough."

"She won't be sympathetic," Clara said. "Of course it isn't the first time someone has been rushed to the hospital like that, but there are certain things she doesn't believe you should take into your own hands."

Meg went to her room, telling herself, "Nana thinks nothing of taking other people's lives in her hands, but being a good Christian and a strong woman she doesn't believe in anticipating God or in human weakness."

She went to bed to lie awake for a time remembering, reliving, rehearing, and then half slept. She knew how to listen through dreams for a voice calling or a bell ringing. The telephone rang shortly before two and Meg stumbled sleepily into the hall. "Charles?" she asked, sitting by the little table there.

"Darling—she's all right. Emergency lived up to its name. I just stayed because she seemed to want me. Besides her parents were in the waiting room; her mother was absolutely distraught."

"It will be kept quiet?" she asked him.

"Who can keep things quiet? We'll do our best. And Mrs. Keble is going to take Sophie to Florida for a while, after she's released, which will be in a day or so. There's an aunt or someone there."

"I'll stop in and see her tomorrow—today, I mean, if it's all right with her doctor."

"Anything you do is all right with Sophie's doctor." She could hear him yawn over the wire and said, "Do get home and get some sleep."

"I'll buzz over to the interns' quarters and beg a hard bed for what's left of the night and release the public booth," he said. "I'll turn up for breakfast at home. You go back to sleep, Meg; and remember, I love you."

"I won't forget."

They both heard the tiny click of an instrument being replaced and Meg hung up. So Cornelia hadn't turned off her phone? I didn't really expect she would, Meg thought, and as Clara's door opened, waved at her, said, "Everything's all right," and returned to bed.

Tomorrow the deluge; meantime she would sleep as long as her alarm clock would permit.

Tomorrow was another day; it always is.

She awoke at the alarm clock's insistence—it had no bell; it simply buzzed like a mammoth and outraged bee—and in the minuscule interval before full consciousness, before she sat up in bed, she was aware of nothing except happiness, like morning sunlight. Then she remembered, and while joy remained, there was also apprehension.

The weekday morning routine was simple. Cornelia breakfasted in bed, at whatever hour she chose to ring for her tray—usually early but not as early as this. Andrew would be stirring, and Clara, and it was time for Meg to shower, to dress, to look in on her son and to go downstairs for toast and coffee. When Meg had first gone to work, Cornelia had suggested she be served at the dining table, but Meg had argued against it. It would be so much easier for Morton and Mrs. Morton if she had her coffee in the kitchen.

So she drank it there this morning, looking out of the windows at the geranium-filled flower boxes and the far blue sky and scudding clouds, and remarking to Mrs. Morton that a fine September was predicted. She had finished her second cup and refused more toast when the bell rang, an indicator fell into place, Mrs. Morton glanced at the clock, and Morton, the tray already assembled, brought Cornelia's small silver coffeepot to the stove.

"I'll be on my way," said Meg, smiled at them and went out. This was D Day, *Der Tag* or whatever. A day like a great many others, a Thursday, and the Mortons' day out. On Thursdays, Cornelia rarely entertained; if compelled to, the Mortons obliged. On Thursdays, if Cornelia was out, Clara and Meg had supper with Andrew; if Cornelia was in, Clara cooked competently with Cornelia contributing little gourmet touches. She fancied herself as an occasional cook and often had told Meg of the hunting cabin they'd once owned in the mountains where she'd cook for her husband and herself, and of the camping trips with him, and later, Andy. "On those trips my men officiated," she said once, "but left me to cope with the washing up."

As Meg drove toward the hospital, thoughts were as spider webs in her mind, crossing, crisscrossing, but forming a sort of definite pattern. She was so absorbed in following the tenuous threads that only a warning shout from a truck driver caused her to brake sharply to avoid running through a red light. "Watch it, sister," he said.

She thanked him, and went on when the light changed. Watch it, sister. The password for the day.

A little after eleven, Charles came charging in. "Where have you——" he began truculently, and she motioned to him to keep his voice down. Mrs. Elgin was in her office, the door was open, they could hear her talking to her secretary.

Meg said, "I was at a meeting."

"Oh, that. See you in the coffee shop. Noon. I've twenty thousand things to do."

He went out and she waited a moment before going on with the desk work, in order to give her heart time to right itself.

They met in the lobby and went into the coffee shop together; as usual it was well occupied, but there was a corner table and Charles made for it. He said, as usual to the young volunteer, "Coffee," and then to Meg, "Five minutes. What happened?"

"Nothing."

"You didn't tell her."

"No. Only that you were going to call me, however late or early and that she should turn her bedroom phone off."

"Which she didn't. I heard the click."

Meg said with a placidity she didn't feel, "I was certain, of course, that she wouldn't. Well, anyway she overheard enough not to be astonished when I talk to her after I get back."

"Better call me."

"I can hardly report by telephone, Charles."

"Why not? Open and above board from now on. Here's the alleged coffee."

He drank, made a face, and said, "This is on you of course," and rose. He looked down smiling, but his eyes were anxious. He said, "Don't let her intimidate you."

"I won't."

"She'll huff and she'll puff, but she can't blow your house down, my house, ours. Call, if you can."

And then he was gone and people were looking after him and at her. She sat and let the coffee cool, feeling a little sick, and finally, seeing one of the supervisors coming toward her, rose.

"Hey, don't dash off," said the older woman. "Stay with me for a few minutes. Gosh, I'm tired and it's just past noon."

"I'm sorry, Jess. I have to see Mrs. Elgin."

"Maybe I'll catch you later for lunch? Did you hear about Sophie Keble?"

But Meg was on her way to the cashier's desk.

She went directly from the coffee shop to Sophie's room. They'd put her in a private room and Meg said to the charge nurse, "Dr. Scott said I could see her."

"Poor kid," remarked the charge nurse. She added, "Her mother's there."

Meg knocked and went in. Sophie was lying against her

118

pillows as white as they and Mrs. Keble was sitting by the bed.

"Hi," said Meg to Sophie and added, "Hello, Mrs. Keble."

"I suppose everyone knows," said Sophie listlessly, and her mother's eyes filled with tears.

"Oh, I doubt that," said Meg and sat down on the straight chair. Mrs. Keble said, as if relieved, "I'll just be in the waiting room," and scurried out.

Sophie said, "There's no use scolding. I told Scotty that after——"

"Did he scold?"

"Not exactly."

"I'm not going to exactly, either. Sophie, if Roger comes through this——"

"If—if," said Sophie and beat her hands on the counterpane.

"He might," said Meg. "He has a chance. Suppose you hadn't been brought here in time, how would he feel when he's released?"

Sophie said, "I don't know. I just didn't want to feel any more, ever. I just wanted to be—nothing."

Meg rose. She said, "You're very young, you have a lot of feeling to do—good, bad, and indifferent—before you're through. And you're selfish, Sophie."

"Selfish?"

"You thought of yourself, and oblivion; not of Roger, not of your parents, not your friends. It takes a certain amount of physical courage," she said reflectively, "to swallow a glass of water and a handful of sleeping pills, and I'm not going to ask how you got them."

"I saved them up," said Sophie defiantly.

"Okay—so you saved them. Yes, it takes courage, but to go on living *and* feeling, that takes guts."

Sophie put out her hand and Meg took it, and the younger woman said, "I suppose so. I'll try." She wasn't pretty this sunny noon; she didn't look much like the girl who had come to the Country Club with Charles recently. She said, "Between you and Scotty." She took her hand away and put it over her eyes. After a moment she whispered, "I'm so ashamed. When I saw my mother and father last night, and again today——"

"You'll be all right."

"Mother's taking me to Florida." She opened her drowned blue eyes and said, "I don't want to go. Suppose—suppose there's news?"

"You'll hear it," said Meg, "even in Florida. It isn't the end of the world. Last night wasn't either. You'll learn."

Then she went back to work and later to lunch with her casual friend, Jess, and finally drove back to the Brand house, to face the end of the day, which would be a beginning.

Ten

MORTON MET HER in the entrance hall and he must have been waiting for her. She had walked from the garage, conscious that it was a little cold, or was the chilly feeling one of apprehension? On the way back from the hospital she had forced her mind away from Cornelia and concentrated it on Sophie, wondering if the trip with her mother would do any good, wondering if anything would, except of course that shopworn but often valid cure-all—time —or Roger's return.

Time worked in various ways; one way was to scar.

Unless Meg was out with Cornelia, or rarely, out alone at night, Morton did not lurk by the door; she came, she went, she was to all intents and purposes one of the family. But for Cornelia's departures and return he was, unless bidden otherwise, as duty bound as if awaiting the changing of the guard.

Now he flickered out of the living room and remarked that it had clouded up and if it rained over the Labor Day weekend, more people than usual would be killed. And, as she agreed with him, added, "Mrs. Brand left word that she would not be home for dinner; but, she won't be late."

"Oh? Thank you, Morton," Meg said and went on upstairs. Cornelia had not mentioned an engagement, as she usually did. She generally said briskly, "I'm going to the So and so's," or, "I have a dinner meeting; you, Andrew and Clara will have to amuse yourselves." But perhaps something had come up suddenly.

She went on to the nursery. It was not yet time for Andrew's bath and supper. She would enjoy both.

"Hi, darling," she said to her son and smiled at Clara. "Cheers," Andrew responded happily, dragging a small wooden train around.

"Now where did that one come from?"

Clara said, "Radio, I think." There might not be a television set in the house, but there was radio; everyone had a radio, and there was a short-wave set in Cornelia's office. Meg rarely turned hers on except for weather, but Clara was —not too secretly—addicted to music and chatter.

Meg sat down in a low chair. It had been, she felt, implicit in Morton's statement that Mrs. Brand would not be late, that she should wait up.

She started to speak, but Andrew interrupted with the air of someone imparting tidings of importance. "Nana went. She said . . ." He hesitated, his span of attention short.

Meg looked at Clara, Clara at Andrew, "Nana said good-by, be a good boy and that she'd come see you when she could," she reminded him.

Andrew's slight scowl of indecision—rather like his mother's in miniature—was replaced by a sunny smile. He said, "Yes," and returned to his train, roaring at it.

"He does talk a lot," said Meg and then, "I didn't know Nana was going out."

"Oh, she had a phone call," Clara said. "Mrs. Ulster, I think, wanted her to come to dinner, just the two of them, and talk over something that's come up."

"Hospital," Meg deduced. Mrs. Ulster was on the Board. She wondered idly: An emergency? She'd heard of none.

Well, perhaps there was one. She said, "Back presently," and went to her room, took a shower, dressed, put on a housecoat and lay down on the bed. In a way, reprieve; in another way, suspense. She thought angrily: I wouldn't put it past her to have gone out on purpose and postponed . . . she knew

I'd have to talk to her this afternoon, or if someone was here, after dinner.

Andrew had his bath and supper. They all had trays upstairs together, as they sometimes did, courtesy of both Mortons. Morton brought sherry for Clara and Meg her small accustomed drink, with a tot of ginger ale and a cherry for Andrew. This also was customary on evenings when Mrs. Brand absented herself.

Afterwards Meg carried two trays down and came back to read to Andrew while Clara took the other and conferred with Mrs. Morton. Then, at Andrew's insistence they played his little record player—nursery rhymes, for the most part—and when he was sleepy, Clara put him to bed.

They went into her room to talk. She said thoughtfully, "You haven't spoken to Mrs. Brand yet?"

"How could I? As far as I know she was asleep when I went down to breakfast."

Clara shrugged her thin shoulders. She said, "She can't put it off forever."

"You think she deliberately——?"

"I don't know," said Clara.

"I'm the one," said Meg, "who'd rather put it off. I hate scenes."

"Mrs. Brand doesn't make scenes—exactly," Clara told her.

"But what can she *do?*" Meg demanded. "I'm free to fall in love, to remarry." She thought of Andy's picture, the informal one she liked best, on her bedside table. She had looked at it often these past few days. The eyes, squinting a little in the sun, and laughing straight at her, had looked back without reproach.

"I don't know," said Clara flatly.

They talked for a while, though neither said anything important; each was making conversation and then Meg rose. She said, "I'll read awhile."

"You could go to bed."

"At this hour? Anyway, I won't postpone it." The condemned man ate a hearty supper she thought. "And I'm restless." She touched Clara's shoulder. "I'll report later," she promised and went back to her room to finish the book she'd started a week before, not knowing what it was all about. Then, after walking about for a time, she went down to the library next to Cornelia's office to hunt up another.

It must have been about nine o'clock when she heard the car drive in. The hall door stood open, but Morton scurried to it mouselike. They heard Cornelia speaking to Ramsay. She said something about airport, at eleven.

Airport?

Cornelia came in, elegant in cocoa brown. She said, "I won't require anything further, Morton, thank you," as if he had offered her champagne and peaches on a silver salver. She smiled at Meg and, as Morton said good night and went off, asked, "Did you have a pleasant evening?"

"Very. Supper with Andrew and Clara. . . . I just came down for a book."

"Did you find one?"

"Yes. . . . Nana, if I could talk to you . . . ?"

Cornelia asked, looking at her with the cool brown eyes, "Is something wrong?" Her regard sharpened. "Andrew——" she began.

"He's fine—no, nothing's wrong, Nana, but——"

"It will have to wait," said Cornelia. "I had an exhausting evening. There are some unfortunate situations at the hospital, one being Sophie Keble. Harriet and I wanted to talk matters over before the next Board meeting. It's possible I'll call a special meeting. Anyway, all that, plus Harriet's penchant for rich food—she's really an excellent cook and this, of course, was spur of the moment—has brought on one of my stupid migraines and I have to fly to Boston in the morning. I'll be away at least overnight."

"It wouldn't take me five minutes to tell you."

"I know what you're going to tell me," said Cornelia equably. "We can discuss it on my return."

She smiled, sun on a glacier and added, "Will you turn off the lights, please, Meg? Morton forgot the outside." She stopped, looked at Meg as if conscious for the first time, of the housecoat, and added, "unless of course you're expecting someone?"

"I'm not expecting anyone," said Meg.

"And this time I'll really turn off my phone," said Cornelia, wielding honesty like a weapon.

She went upstairs, saying, "I'll see you when I return and of course I'll telephone from Boston. Clara knows where I stay—the hotel, I mean. I'm not going to Cousin Olive's."

She went on upstairs. Meg took the book she had selected at random, turned off the outside lights, locked up, turned off the downstairs lights except those which illuminated the stairs and which could be switched off from the hall. She passed through and shut firmly the little gate at the top, then knocked at Clara's door. Clara was sitting up with the local newspaper in her hands and her radio playing softly.

"I didn't know you liked rock and roll," said Meg, coming in.

"I don't. But I have to keep up with the times."

Meg shut the door. She said, "Nana's off to Boston tomorrow, by air."

"Her cousin? I knew she was ailing, but then she always is."

"No, she's not staying at the Wards'; she said you'd know the hotel. Anyway, she'll call tomorrow."

"When's she leaving?"

"For the airport, at eleven, from here."

"Then you didn't have a chance to tell her?"

"Oh, she knows," said Meg wearily. "She practically told me she'd listened on her extension last night. She seems to think we could discuss it later. What's in Boston? I don't think she's been there half a dozen times since I came here."

"Oh, the cousins, a raft of them; not that she'd give any of them the time of day if she had two watches and both of them running, except of course Olive Paterson. Also the Brand lawyers."

Meg said startled, "But I thought that Perry and Perry——"

"Oh, yes, here in the town; but the Boston firm has always looked after some aspects of the business. I wouldn't know what."

It occurred to Meg that tomorrow was Friday, the start of the weekend. Even for Cornelia lawyers would not huddle waiting in their offices; they'd be off to the Cape, or Marble-head, or wherever.

After a while she went back into the hall, sat down at the telephone table, looked in the local book and then dialed the Scott home.

Sarah answered, Meg identified herself and Sarah said Dr. Charles was at the hospital and Dr. and Mrs. Scott were out to dinner with friends. "Is there a message, Mrs. Brand?" she asked.

"No. . . . Wait. . . . Yes, please would you ask Dr. Charles to call me when he comes in?"

"I will. How's Clara?"

"Fine," said Meg. "Want to ask her yourself?"

Sarah agreed that would be nice, so Meg went to fetch Clara. She said, "I called Charles. He's out; so are his parents, but Sarah would like to speak to you."

Clara said, "Perhaps Mrs. Brand will need to use the telephone."

"I don't think so," said Meg. "Tonight I believe we can both talk all night to anyone at all."

Clara gave her a quizzical look. She then said, resigned, "Gossip, I guess. Well, maybe that's what I need."

When Charles called about eleven and Meg answered, he said, "Just got in. Sarah left me a note. What's up, darling?"

"Nothing. Or the balloon, I don't know. Nana was out when I came back from work and when she returned, she went right to bed, with a headache. And she's going to Boston tomorrow. I'll see you at the hospital."

Charles said, "Okay. Look, over the weekend several of us are taking turns in emergency because they'll need extra hands. I've drawn Sunday night. Let's drop in on Bassett about nine tomorrow night for a pint and a council of war."

On Friday the emergencies started early, people tearing off to enjoy themselves and encountering obstacles like stone walls or hostile mobile ones. There was an uproar in Maternity with the arrival of twins, prematurely. Mrs. Elgin had masses of paper work to pass along to her assistant. And Meg saw Charles only as she was leaving for home.

He said, "Nine then," and waved at her in the lobby. She went out to the car, headed for the Brand house, Andrew, Clara, and supper trays.

They were finishing, listening to Andrew's account of an experience he and Bunny had had, "under bed," he said spreading his arms wide, "big—big as this house, and black," when the telephone rang and they heard Morton take the call downstairs. Meg went to lean over the little gate. "Is it for me, Morton?" she asked.

"It's for Clara," said Morton, "from Boston, Mrs. Brand."

Clara took the call upstairs. She said, "Yes," several times and then, "Of course," and then, "Yes, I have his number," and finally, "Yes, Mrs. Brand, I'll get Andrew."

But Meg, listening, had him in her arms in the hall and Clara said, "His Nana wants to speak to him."

"Nana," howled Andrew. If she spoke, he did not listen. It was his first experience with the genius of Alexander Graham Bell. "Nana," he waved the instrument, he shouted, "Hello."

Finally Clara took the telephone away and he collapsed into tears of rage. Where was Nana? Why couldn't he see her? She had said, "Hello."

"That's all right, Mrs. Brand," said Clara. "He's just upset because he could hear you, but couldn't see you."

Back in Andrew's room, after he had consented to be pacified, she said, "She didn't realize this is the Labor Day weekend."

In a pig's ear she didn't, Meg thought.

"So she couldn't see the people she wanted to see," Clara went on, poker-faced, "and is going, tomorrow morning, with Mrs. Paterson and her daughter to Chatham. She gave me the number. She'll be back Wednesday."

Meg said suddenly. "Fine, I'm going out with Charles for a while, tomorrow night."

"Ask him here sometime when Andrew can see him," Clara suggested placidly.

It was quite a weekend. Charles came the next evening to pick Meg up and they went to Bassett's for their pint. "I haven't had time to eat," Charles said crossly. "How about you?"

"I wasn't hungry. Andrew had supper downstairs in the dining room in his high chair. It was an occasion, very nervous making."

"Then two steak sandwiches rare," said Charles. "Got to get our protein. And coffee. . . . Now, what's up?"

"You asked me that before. Nothing that I know of except that Nana never has charged off to Boston or the Cape or anywhere else without a week of preparation, or not since I've been in Melton. She said she wasn't going to stay with her cousins."

"The Patersons."

"You know them?"

"Slightly. Andy once had something going with one of the young ones, I forget her name. His mother disapproved.

It was a long time ago, he was maybe sixteen. . . . Did you look in her closet?"

"Whose closet for heaven's sake? . . . Oh, Nana's? No, of course not. Why would I?"

"To see if she took Cape Cod clothes along; she'd want something other than city things, idiot."

"You think she knew before?"

Charles said, "Use your beautiful redhead. No one forgets a Labor Day weekend; fun, games, celebrations, accidents, the papers have been full of it for a week. Warnings, statistics; and a little political hanky-panky here and there, speeches and such. Every time Cornelia Brand looked at a paper, any paper, or at her calendar or turned on a radio, she'd know. Sure, I think she planned it."

"Since when?"

"Since Wednesday night, Love."

"But, why?"

"No Sherlock, he," Charles said. "It just seems to the enfeebled mind of the great Dr. Scott that your mother-in-law is going to keep you in ignorance of her ideas, motives, and machinations for a little longer. Forget it. You'll find out in due time and I'll be around when and if you need me. I'll even go down on one knee and ask your hand in matrimony."

She laughed. The steak sandwiches came and Charles said, "Talk about us. We, too, have plans. How'd you like to go to England?"

"England?" She dropped her knife.

"Close your mouth. You look like a pretty fish—a gold fish, I think. Why not? If I can get away for a couple of weeks, we can make it by jet; you can see your people; Andrew can meet them for the first time."

"But I don't rate a vacation."

"We'll manage. You can always resign. Not that I want you to. I rather like the idea of having a working wife. . . . Well, even if we had a week—I bet your aunt would take

Andrew on like a shot and give us a few days to ourselves, and then when we come back——"

She said, "Wait a minute. I can't keep up with you. When is all this to take place?"

He said, "How about late October? Nice anywhere in the temperate zone. . . . Did you know I owned a house?"

"No."

"I do. My grandmother left it to me. It's old and I like it. I'll take you there one of these days. It's rented, but the people are leaving October first. A job transfer. If you reach for the gold ring, as a young executive, you must get on the merry-go-round. Meg, do you think Clara would come to us?"

She said, troubled, "No, Charles, and how I wish it—but she owes so much to the Brands."

"To Cornelia, you mean? . . . Yes, I know about the old mother in the costly nursing home. I go to see her now and then." He grinned, and all the sparkle was there. "She's rather fond of me, and so is Clara, but of course if someone has to be sent for, it's Dr. Foster. Nana calls the tune."

She said, "For Clara to leave Nana seems out of the question to me, although it disturbs me because Andrew is so attached to her."

"We'll manage somehow. Well, let's see. There's ample room in the old oaken homestead for us, Andrew, and a couple more besides, but that's not for us. We have to be on our own. By the way, can you cook?"

"Of course," she said indignantly.

"How was I to know? Consider the lilies of the field. I am not asking how well, mind you. I'll find out someday; at the moment I don't care. You tell Aunt Cornelia we're going to be married in October once the hospital arrangements and my practice are squared away and we can set the date. Church?"

She nodded and felt a ridiculous impulse to cry.

"That will please Mom. As for the rest, if Madame Brand

throws you out, as I've said before, we'll take you in with your infant in your arms. No snow, however," he added thoughtfully.

"And not much of an infant."

"No. . . . Meg, wouldn't you like me to be there when you explain the itinerary?"

"No, I'd rather you weren't."

"I can always hide behind a clipped hedge and hoot like an owl."

"Darling, be serious. It's mostly your plan to take us to England which worries me. It's wonderful of course, but that will upset her most of all," she said unhappily.

"I know. But it's only for, say, ten days, two weeks at the most, and then we'll be home and she'll have—what do you call them?—visiting privileges."

Meg sighed. She said, "I'd give almost anything to see my aunt and her husband and to have them see Andrew."

"You don't have to give anything but yourself, which reminds me, I have here a small token of my esteem."

He produced a jeweler's box, which Meg opened. The diamond, not too big and not too small, was of fine quality, clarity, and color. And Charles said, "It was one of Mom's; she gave it to me a long while ago. I had it reset."

She said, "But you haven't had time really and I didn't say until recently that I'd marry you."

"I had it reset shortly after I met you. I knew I was out of my mind, but I enjoyed the lunacy. Put it on. . . . No, I suppose I should, but maybe Bassett's isn't the ideal environment."

Meg closed the box. She said, "I love it, and you. Please keep it a little longer for me, Charles, until everything's settled."

She put the box in his hand, which closed over it, and hers. He said, "Okay, solemn ceremony later." He looked at her left hand; she was wearing only her wedding ring. He remembered the aquamarine and said with more diffidence than she'd ever seen him display, "I don't have Andy's imagination, Meg."

"No," she agreed, "not his, but your own."

They smiled at each other and Bassett, on his way to the bar, nodded. His kind of people. He wished them well. He'd drink to that when the last patron had departed. Now he simply came back with some splendid brandy in correct snifters. He said—and this time he did drop his h's—"To your very good 'ealth, it's on the 'ouse."

So they toasted him and each other and laughed. The brandy was warming and what was between them was warming also, a flame but not a destructive one; a flame to warm their hearts and minds and bodies, a flame which was also a light. No matter what, thought Meg.

Eleven

D RIVING HOME from work, a little late, on Tuesday,
Meg reflected that tomorrow Cornelia would be home
from the Cape, and the usual routine would again
assert itself. No, not routine, for once Cornelia was in resi-
dence again, Meg would try to discuss her plans. But since
her departure, coming home had been almost like really coming home, with only the Mortons, Andrew, and Clara there;
and Meg's time her own, as it had been Saturday evening.
She had seen very little of Charles since: Sunday, in her
office, for a few minutes; Monday, at the coffee shop; not at
all today, not even a chance encounter. She thought: Tomorrow is his day off; perhaps we can be together, somewhere during the evening. By that time Nana will be home
and I'll have talked with her. She thought further: And
when I see Charles my head will be bloody but unbowed.

She was laughing a little, inwardly. Charles and his
quotations! She'd asked him once, "Why?" and he'd replied
seriously, "I like to read, I have a catholic taste in literature,
also a retentive memory, and once I wanted to be a writer."

This had astonished her and he'd said with some asperity,
"Other medical gentlemen have made it, and been so success-
ful that medicine went down the drain except as background.
But," he added, "I have no talent, none whatsoever."

She'd asked, "Why, then, the earlier aspirations?" And
he'd said, "Andy, of course. He always had the ears and eyes

of a born reporter; also imagination and the gift of the right words in the right paragraphs. Don't worry, darling, I recovered from the fever in prep school."

As she negotiated the driveway, she saw Charles's familiar somewhat beat-up car parked in front of the house. Andrew? No, she reassured herself; Clara would have called Dr. Jarvis. She put her own car in the garage, walked quickly to the house and went in. It was quiet downstairs, but she heard voices, laughter, and curious thumpings coming from above.

She ran up the stairs and into the nursery, where Charles and Andrew were crawling about the floor in pursuit of a small green object, which jumped nervously. Charles had in his hand the little bulb, on the end of a cord, which made it perform. He waved at her with the other hand. "Hi, darling," he said and Andrew parroted, "Hi, darling." He sat back on his heels and pointed to the object. "Frog," he happily explained.

In a corner the dilapidated rabbit sulked, while Clara, sitting in the big chair, looked up smiling from her knitting.

"What kept you?" Charles asked.

"The usual. What are you doing here?"

"Made my last house call, have a little time before the hospital, thought maybe someone would feed me."

"Discipline's out the window. No bath so far, no supper," Clara remarked unperturbed.

"Poor us," said Charles sadly and Andrew burst into laughter.

Meg sat down on an ottoman. "Charles, if you bewitch Andrew into a tub——" she began.

"Be-warlock," he corrected her. "Always mind your genders."

"Then," she went on, paying no attention, "I'll persuade Mrs. Morton to serve supper for us in the dining room."

She left Charles and Clara to cajole Andrew and went downstairs to consult the Mortons. Mrs. Morton was delighted; she had a well-stocked larder and nothing offered as much challenge as what she called a scratch meal. The high chair would emerge and Morton, Meg decided, would serve their drinks at the table rather than in the living room. Sherry, for Clara and herself, Scotch on the rocks, for their guest.

She went back upstairs to observe the ritual of the bath at which Charles was busily presiding. He was chasing the menagerie around the tub; the frog had been added to it; Andrew was splashing; Charles was wet.

When all this was over, they went downstairs, Andrew in his diminutive night gear, robe, and slippers, and Charles without jacket or tie. Clara assured him the jacket would dry, she'd hang it up, also the tie, which she would later iron.

Meg had changed to a jersey frock and Charles said, "Maybe I should eat in the kitchen?"

Morton beamed, drinks were served, including the ginger ale plus cherry for Andrew and there was clear soup, wonderful cold beef, hot green beans, and a salad.

For dessert—because Andrew loved it and it had been planned for his nursery supper—rice pudding; there was also milk to supplement Andrew's fare, coffee for the adults.

At that stage—what with laughter, clanging of spoons, and admonishments from Clara—no one heard a car drive up until Morton, possibly through ESP, became aware of a stirring in the entrance hall. Nearly dropping whatever it was he carried, he hurried out.

Cornelia's voice was distinct. She said, "Good evening, Morton. Will you please take the luggage upstairs; Mrs. Paterson will have the pink room and Mrs. Dayton, the yellow."

She then walked into the dining room, followed by two women, her cousin Olive, and Olive's daughter, Jean.

"Well," said Cornelia, "what fun to find you all here!" As Charles rose, she smiled, asking, "What happened to you, Charles? Were you in an accident or something?" and Charles said, no he'd been halfway in the tub with Andrew.

Meg and Clara knew Olive, and her daughter Jean was

introduced to Meg. Jean cast herself upon Charles, exclaiming that it was wonderful to see him after all these years, and Olive remarked pleasantly that he'd changed. "But haven't we all?" she inquired.

Mrs. Morton made an unaccustomed entrance from the kitchen. She said, "We didn't expect you, Mrs. Brand."

"Of course not," said Cornelia negligently. "When Morton returns, he can clear away and set the table again. . . . How's my boy?" she asked, scooping up Andrew, who having been overlooked, and being overtired, was voicing his disapproval. "It's all right," Cornelia soothed him. "Nana's home now." She then exhibited him to Olive, who was about her own age, a thin, frail woman with the stamp of dissatisfaction upon every feature, and to Jean, about Charles's age and pretty in an enameled fashion.

Both remarked how he'd grown and chucked him under the chin in the humiliating manner of grownups who aren't really interested.

"I'll take him upstairs, Mrs. Brand, he's getting sleepy," Clara suggested.

"Too much bathtub," suggested Andrew's Nana. She spoke to her cousins, "Come on upstairs too, girls," she said. "It will give Mrs. Morton time to fix something for us, and Meg and Charles an opportunity to recover from our sudden appearance." She herded the ladies from the room saying, "Don't wait for us, you two. Mrs. Morton will provide something. It was a tiring drive, actually, and we stopped for a too-lavish lunch."

Miraculously, the room cleared. Morton and his wife were again in the kitchen, and Meg and Charles looked at each other.

"Well," said Charles, "I feel rather as if we'd been caught *in flagrante delicto* or whatever it is——"

"She was to return tomorrow," Meg said, "and she didn't phone to have Ramsay meet her. How did she *get* here?"

"I'd say by six-o'clock broom. She'll say in the costly Paterson car; probably Jean drove. Nip upstairs, Love, and retrieve my damp coat and wrecked tie and I'll depart."

"Coward!"

"No. Remember the one about he who lives to run away? In any case I haven't yet been passed by the membership committee, so no family reunions for me. Make it snappy."

Meg flew upstairs, disregarding open doors, got the jacket and the tie, flew down again, and went with Charles to his car. He said, "My apologies and all that. I hurried out on a mercy errand. Actually, I do have a couple of hospital patients to see." He put his arm around her heedless of the fact that there might be one, two or even three pairs of eyes watching from the upstairs windows. He said, "Andy would never know Jean—that was the cousin he once fancied. Maybe if she washed her face, I could see a remote resemblance." At the car he kissed her, without haste. "Remember tomorrow's my alleged day off. I'll call you at the hospital. I can't wait to hear what happens in this installment. Trust Auntie to hang us over the cliff," he said.

When Meg returned to the house, all signs of their supper had vanished except for her coffee cup. "It's cold, perhaps you wish more, Mrs. Brand," Morton said, as he reset the table.

She shook her head, drank the tepid remainder thoughtfully and presently heard laughter and footsteps. Cornelia came in with her guests and Meg got to her feet. "If only we'd known——" she began.

"Ah, but you didn't," said Cornelia and indicated the chairs on either side of her. She said to Morton, "We may as well have cocktails here. Martinis," she decided. "That will give Mrs. Morton more time—I hope she has something light for us."

"Light but nourishing, Mrs. Brand," he assured her.

Olive said to Meg, "I'd expected Cornelia to stay till tomorrow, drive back to Boston with us and fly home, perhaps

Thursday. She had an appointment today, but she broke it."

"Suited me," said Jean. "The Cape was heaven, but I have a session Friday with my doctor and it seemed fun to come here for the night."

She'd been married, was childless, now divorced, and the appointment was with her psychiatrist. Meg had heard Cornelia mention "poor Jean" a time or two. She seemed to be holding up well. Perhaps she'd made the usual transference?

Drinks came and Jean wolfed hers as if gin were going to be rationed and remarked, "Scotty's much better-looking than he used to be in my younger days, but then I had eyes only for Andy. If you hadn't spoken of Scotty's car parked outside, when we drove in, I mightn't have known him, Cousin Cornelia."

Mrs. Morton had risen to the occasion, clear hot broth, a very gourmet mushroom omelet, and a newly tossed salad.

"Wonderful," Olive murmured languidly, and Jean said, "I thought I'd never eat again after that lunch." Meg remarked, "If you'd phoned us, Nana. . . ."

"Why?" asked Cornelia with some asperity. "I didn't need anyone to meet me. There's ample food in the house and the guest rooms are always in readiness. It was all very spur of the moment; we simply got in the car and drove off."

Dessert was not rice pudding but fresh fruit, crackers and cheese, after which they went into the living room for coffee and Meg sat and listened to Jean complain—she was a talented complainer—and to Olive's organ recital, aimed mostly at Meg's professional ears. Olive's health was her major topic of conversation; Cornelia had once said she could run through a dozen doctors in half a dozen years. She also listened to Cornelia's comments on Boston. "Hot, and all the people escaping for the weekend, as we did. The Cape was beautiful. Hundreds of trippers, of course, but you can't really spoil natural beauty no matter who's sprawled on the sand or crashing around the dunes."

After a while Meg rose. She asked, "Will you excuse me now? I hope I'll see you tomorrow when I get back from work."

Olive said no, they'd have to leave after lunch, so Meg shook hands and went on upstairs. As usual she stopped in Clara's room.

"Andrew asleep?"

"Fell into bed as if pole-axed. Charles gave him quite a workout. It didn't hurt; it's good for him."

"I wonder why Nana——" Meg began and then stopped. It was none of her business, really, why Cornelia had been seized by a whim and acted upon it.

"I dunno," said Clara. "It's not like her; she likes everything planned ahead and orderly."

"But she could have telephoned from the Cape, or from wherever they had lunch."

"Yes," Clara agreed. "You look tired. Isn't Charles fine with Andrew? He was heartbroken because Charles didn't come to tuck him and Bunny in. Mrs. Brand and her cousins will be up late if they follow their usual routine. Go to bed, or you may be tapped for bridge."

"As I recall it from other visits, Mrs. Paterson isn't usually an early riser, though she must have been today," said Meg. "In any case, I am, being a working woman."

"I hope you won't be, for long," Clara said.

"That depends on a lot of things, mostly Andrew," Meg told her. "We'll just have to work it out."

"You've really made plans?"

"Charles has. They seem—oh—wonderful and wild. But I can't tell you yet——"

"That's all right," Clara said, a little stiffly.

"It isn't that," said Meg quickly. "I'd trust you with my life as well as Andrew's. Perhaps I'm superstitious. But if you talk about things before everything's—well—straightened out, maybe they won't happen."

She thought: I never stopped talking about Andy in the

brief time before we were married, yet we were married, just as he'd planned. But after that . . . ?

Clara said, "Well, you'll tell me in time." She hesitated, "Maybe I can help."

"You're not trying to tell me you'd leave here?"

Clara said carefully, "It's possible, if you and Charles want me. We'll see."

"But, of course, we want you." Meg's face was bright with astonishment.

"I have to work things out, too," Clara said.

Meg thought: It's too good to be true. Clara going to England with them, providing Andrew's security. Clara returning to stay with them in Charles's as yet unknown house.

Clara said, "When you talk to Mrs. Brand, I'd rather you didn't say anything about me—not until I've figured things out, Meg."

"If I ever talk to her," said Meg. "She seems determined not to be alone with me for even five minutes. Good night—and you've helped already. Andrew needs you so much."

Clara nodded. "For a while anyway, until he's off to school." Her face was shadowed, and her voice unsteady. She said, squaring her thin shoulders and smiling, "But we won't think about that yet."

Meg woke, toward midnight, and heard voices and footsteps in the hall. She hadn't been summoned to the bridge table, after all. She'd read, and thought, and dreamed, first waking, then sleeping. Now she went back to sleep until the alarm clock buzzed.

In the morning she was aware, as she entered the kitchen, that the Mortons had been in conference, probably over last night. Morton and his wife had been with Cornelia for a long time and had doubtless spent most of the night discussing her unusual behavior. But all Mrs. Morton said to Meg about it was she did hope everything had been all right last evening.

Meg reassured her.

"It was sort of upsetting," admitted Mrs. Morton, "everything happening so unexpected."

Morton was busy setting up three trays and as Meg drank her coffee—"I fixed an egg, Mrs. Brand. You didn't have much last night," said Mrs. Morton.

"Tons," said Meg, but ate the poached egg, drank her juice, and was on her way. As she left the kitchen, she heard the buzzer sound. That would be Cornelia, she thought, not Olive or her daughter.

Charles called her, midmorning.

"Busy?"

"Naturally. Good morning."

"Anything to report, or can't you?"

"I went to bed early. The others stayed downstairs, but I did talk with Clara."

"About plans?"

"Not yet. I think she has a plan of her own." Someone knocked at Meg's door and she said, "I'm sorry, I have to hang up now."

Dr. Meadows wandered in, and waited patiently.

"Wait a minute," said Charles. "What about tonight?"

"No. Tonight is, I hope, D-day." She hung up and asked Dr. Meadows, "What can I do for you?"

Cornelia was not in when Meg returned. She'd gone out, Morton reported, shortly after her guests left, but would return for tea. She did, with Mr. Jones, the minister, and his wife. Meg, having changed, was invited to drink tea and listen. It seemed Andrew was not on exhibition. Clara had said that Mrs. Brand had suggested that he have an early bath, supper, and bed. Meg stayed with them briefly and then returned to Cornelia, and when the kind, colorless Joneses had departed asked, "May I talk to you before dinner, Nana?"

Cornelia said, "Can it wait until afterward? I'm more tired than I suspected—all that driving and then staying up late with Olive and Jean, and getting them off after lunch. After that I had an errand which couldn't wait, so I rushed through that, and as I'd already asked the Joneses . . ." She smiled and said, "I must be getting old."

Meg thought: Ten to one she didn't ask the Joneses until this morning or later. Anger was a small, hot flame, and nothing feeds it like frustration. She said, "All right, after dinner then. It's—important to me, Nana."

"Of course," said Cornelia soothingly.

Clara was with them at dinner. She could hear Andrew if he called or even stirred. Cornelia remarked that she was sorry he couldn't have been brought down to see the Joneses. "But he does get overexcited," she added, "and I felt he'd better have a quiet time. He's so high-strung," she added, as if accusingly.

Meg said she didn't think so; he appeared to her to be a perfectly normal child, and all children his age got overexcited or overtired at times.

Finally dinner was over. Meg had not eaten much—a fact Cornelia commented upon—nor, for that matter, had Clara. Cornelia, however, did justice to Mrs. Morton. Meg felt a little lightheaded; perhaps from the martini, which usually she avoided. This drop-by-drop Chinese-torture bit did not agree with her. But it couldn't go on forever. Nor did it.

When Clara had left to go upstairs and Morton had removed the coffee things, Cornelia settled down in a corner of the couch, putting a pillow behind her back and saying, "Irene drives both fast and recklessly, especially around corners. One feels it in one's bones even the day afterward. . . . You are, I presume, going to tell me about you and Charles?"

"Yes," said Meg, her heart steadying.

"You don't have to, you know," said Cornelia. "It's perfectly obvious how matters stand between you. But I do commend your honesty which," she added thoughtfully, "I suppose you owe, however difficult."

Meg said, "I know you don't like Charles, Nana."

The eyebrow went up. Then said Cornelia, "You know more than I do. I've always been fond of him—at least I was, when he was younger, and I don't dislike him now, Meg, I assure you."

"Then you have no objection——?"

Cornelia interrupted. "Naturally I object, but then I'm not of your generation, for which I often thank God—this appalling break down of moral fiber which I see all around me——" She broke off and then said, "I didn't expect you to remain faithful to Andy for the rest of your life, although I must say I expected you to respect his memory for a somewhat longer period. But I realize that you are a young, healthy woman, and therefore," she added distastefully, "concerned with—or rather, troubled by—sex. From my standpoint it's unfortunate that your interest is centered in Charles Scott, an interest which must be as plain to everyone in the hospital as it is to me. I've even heard a little about it, secondhand. I insist on one thing only, which is that this affair be conducted with utmost discretion, and that Charles will no longer come to this house."

Anger can cause tears or laughter, or a sharp surge of violence; you can cry, you can laugh, you can pick up a heavy ash tray . . .

Meg laughed. She said, "Affair, Nana?"

"I daresay that's a rather passé word," said Cornelia evenly, "judging by some of the current fiction I've tried to read."

Meg said, "Let's bring it up to date then. You believe I am sleeping with Charles?"

"If you prefer to put it that way," said Cornelia, who felt physically sick as she said it, "yes; or, if not yet, planning to."

Meg said, "I'm not sleeping with him. But I do plan to; we're going to be married, Nana. That's what I wanted to tell you."

Cornelia went sallow white under her delicate make-up. She said, "You and Charles? I don't believe it."

"It's true," said Meg, "and quite Victorian. He proposed, I accepted."

Cornelia said, "Either you've lost your mind or I have. I simply will not allow it."

"You have no choice. I can marry whom I please," said Meg, "when I please. Andy," she added, "would not have wished me to——"

"Don't bring Andy into this," said Cornelia. Her eyes were hard and bright.

"You're trying to say that you would countenance an affair as long as it wasn't conducted within your sight and hearing, but not my marriage to Charles?" Meg asked.

Cornelia said, "That's one way of putting it, I daresay. And I wish Andy's infatuation had gone no further than——" she broke off and said wearily, "No that's not true, since he left me Andrew."

Meg said quietly, "Andy and I were deeply in love, briefly engaged, briefly married. There was no question of any other relationship between us; and there isn't with Charles. We love each other, and we are going to be married. It's as simple as that."

"Has Charles discussed this with his parents?"

"I don't know, but I expect so. I haven't asked him."

"I see. . . . You have made plans?"

"Charles has. The house he owns will be vacant the first of October. He must, of course, arrange for someone to cover his practice. He wants to be married the end of next month, if possible, and to take us for a short visit to England."

"Us?" repeated Cornelia. Her breathing was shallow and rapid.

"Andrew and me."

There followed what seemed to Meg a long silence. She broke it. "I'm sorry you feel this way, Nana," she said.

Cornelia rose abruptly. "It's kind of you to be concerned with how I feel which is, at the moment, ill. I cannot discuss this further tonight."

Her color was dreadful. She staggered a little walking away, and Meg went quickly to take her arm and ask, "Please let me help you."

Cornelia shook her off. She said, "Don't bother. I'll call Clara." On the stairs she turned. She said, "This discussion is by no means finished. I'll try to talk to you tomorrow."

Twelve

H ALF STUNNED, Meg stayed where she was. She heard
Cornelia knock on Clara's door, she heard lowered
voices, footsteps, and Cornelia's door, shutting. After
a while she took a coat from the hall closet and went outside.
If Cornelia was ill, Clara would call her doctor, she thought,
unless Nana says not to, which she probably would. But not
if Dr. Foster has to come, she'd never permit herself to let
him make an educated guess.

She thought: I wish I could call Charles, but she couldn't.
Cornelia was not so ill that she couldn't pick up the extension.
She thought: I could get in the car and . . .

And what? Drive to the Scotts', ask to see Charles? That,
too, was not possible. And whose car was it? Cornelia's, of
course. Everything was Cornelia's: this house, the food they
ate, and Andrew's Clara.

Meg kept telling herself stubbornly that Cornelia couldn't
do anything; she couldn't kidnap Andrew, she couldn't prevent
Meg from marrying, from taking Andrew with her, or from
going to England, Outer Mongolia, or anywhere else. All
this would pass; everything did.

Still she was crying, sobbing under her breath, the tears
running down her cheeks. She thought: Nana's not rational.
No matter how much she hates the Scotts or for what reason,
no matter how much she hates me . . . it goes beyond that.

She pushed the thought away; it frightened her.

After a while, in control again, she went back into the house and upstairs. She did not stop at Clara's door. For all she knew Clara might still be with Cornelia and, even if she were not, this was definitely not the time for confidences, questions, and answers—if there were answers.

Once in bed, she lay awake for some time and the muted knock at her door startled her. She asked, "Who is it?" and Clara came in. "Just me," she said. "Mrs. Brand is asleep. I fixed some hot milk for her, and she took a sleeping pill. I stayed until she drowsed off."

"If she hears you in here . . ." Meg warned.

"She won't. I put a shot of whiskey in the milk; she takes that sometimes, with the pill. You get some sleep, now."

"Clara, everything's so absurd and so upsetting——"

"I know."

"She told you?"

"No. She simply said she felt ill, that it was probably fatigue, and she'd be all right if she could sleep. But I figured that you'd spoken to her."

"I didn't get very far."

"Sleep on it," Clara advised. "Here, let me fix your pillows."

She did so and went out, closing the door quietly. She had been like a shadow in the room even when Meg turned on the bedside lamp, a gray, confronting shadow.

Meg thought: I wish I dared to take a sleeping pill.

In the morning she went in to see Andrew who was lively and garrulous. Clara looked at her, "Guess you didn't sleep much," she remarked.

"No, but I'll make up for it," said Meg.

Fortunately, there was considerable extra work waiting for her at the hospital. Mrs. Elgin had an appointment with her dentist, so Meg managed scheduled interviews with applicants for the new Licensed Practical Nurse program. She went into the coffee shop for lunch and two of the younger nurses beckoned her to their table. She listened while they discussed one of the interns who had had a drinking problem, and was now, as they said, arrested.

"He was always a drip," said one of the girls, "but now he's a dry drip."

This struck them as hilarious and Meg smiled, knowing some response was expected of her. One girl said, "Well he never turned me on; not like Scotty—ouch!"

It was evident that her friend had kicked her smartly on the shin, whether because Meg was there or because Charles was making his way to the table Meg could not decide. He looked down at them with benevolence. "Gossiping?" he inquired, and the prettier girl said, "Naturally."

"About whom?"

"You, Doctor."

"Good." He looked at Meg and said, "You look terrible."

"Thanks."

"On your way home," he said, "better stop in at the office." He lifted a hand, dropped it, said, " 'Bye, girls," and went on to another table at which one of the residents was having coffee.

Maybe I do look terrible, Meg thought, but maybe he simply wants to talk to me.

She had never been to his office, the one he'd taken over from his father. For years William Scott's office had been in his house, but since Meg had come to Melton he'd been in the Medical Arts Building in the town. She knew his nurse, Miss Weston, whom Charles had inherited. She was a graduate of Massachusetts General and lived, Meg vaguely recalled, with an ancient mother in an apartment on one of Melton's quiet residential streets.

Meg went to the office after work, blessing Charles for the opportunity he had afforded her. She knew the building, a neat modern structure which accommodated three doctors, and a dentist and had ample parking space behind it.

The waiting room was cheerful, with plants, big chairs, a couch, and the usual magazines. There were paintings on the walls and a receptionist back of a curved counter on which there were four telephones. Meg approached her and said, "I'm Mrs. Brand—I believe Dr. Scott is expecting me."

The girl regarded her pleasantly. She said, "If you'll sit down, Mrs. Brand, I'll tell Dr. Scott you're here." She pressed a button, picked up a phone and spoke into it.

There were other people in the waiting room: two elderly women, whispering, turning over the pages of magazines; a woman with a child. Meg remembered that Tom Jarvis' office was also here, but she'd never had occasion to bring Andrew to him; he had always come to Andrew.

Presently Miss Weston emerged and said, "Good afternoon, Mrs. Brand. Dr. Scott will see you now."

It was rather like a stately dream. Meg followed Miss Weston down a corridor. William Scott's name was on a door and his son's also. It was, Charles had once said, an efficient setup. Miss Weston occupied a small anteroom, with files, desk, typewriter, and a telephone. All patients waited in the common reception room and somewhere, Meg knew, there was an X-ray and EKG room, and a laboratory shared by the tenants.

Beyond Miss Weston's cubbyhole were Charles's examination room and office from which he now erupted saying, "Hi," cheerfully and beckoning her in. She obeyed, he shut the door, and Miss Weston's typewriter clattered.

"Do you always keep her this late?"

"When necessary. We've emergencies sometimes," said Charles, "and sometimes, as now, I need a chaperone. Only it isn't after hours tonight. I'm open for business till six."

"You knew I'd come?"

"Of course."

"Just like a regular appointment," said Meg, relaxing a little. Just to be in the room with him steadied her nerves, and at the same time accelerated her pulse. "Since when have you been my doctor?"

He ignored that. He said, "Sit down, darling," and himself sat at the desk facing her. "I wasn't kidding or drumming up trade. You look lousy."

"I couldn't telephone you," she said miserably, "and I was awake half the night."

"What happened?"

She told him and he listened in silence. "I sometimes think she actually hates me," Meg said.

"Oh, I don't think she does, although I'm sure she doesn't like you very much. She might have if you hadn't married Andy. No. It's the situation she hates." He frowned and then, to her astonishment, laughed.

"It isn't funny," she said indignantly.

"No. But how remarkably Aunt Cornelia—the image of virtue, the model of rectitude—is tolerant to a degree of illicit goings on as long as she doesn't have to audition them. If I'd realized that, I wouldn't have offered to make an honest woman of you."

"That hardly describes——" she began crossly, but he was laughing again. She said, "Charles, she's really ill."

"Not seriously. Of course her pressure's high. Foster spoke of it to me once—I don't think she is a docile patient—but apparently not alarmingly so. Anyway, I'd say that she probably worked herself up into something of a snit."

"I don't mean that. I mean, she isn't rational."

He looked at her, a long level look and said, "I wondered when you'd reach that conclusion."

Meg shrank in her chair. She said after a moment, "Andrew."

"Stop shaking. Andrew's all right. As far as I know there's no history of mental illness in the Brand or Melton families. But there's a little madness in all families somewhere, Meg—yours probably, mine, anyone's—Oh, just a touch here and there, an eccentric, a compulsive gambler, an alcoholic," he said resolutely, "or someone senile." He shrugged. "You know it all as well as I do. Cornelia Brand's as rational as most people except on a couple of subjects. That's the way most of us are. In her case, it's power madness; she's trigger happy, she rides shotgun, whatever you want to call it. Even as a kid I could see a little beyond the façade. She can't endure being crossed, or defeated."

"Yes, I know."

He said, "I think I'd better turn up tomorrow."

"It would only make things worse. I'll manage. This is between her and me, Charles."

"Not entirely."

"Well, for now at any rate."

He rose, and leaned to kiss her quickly. "If I gave you a sedative or sleeping pills, would you take them?" he asked.

"No."

"I thought as much. When will I see you?"

"Perhaps Saturday; I'm off," she said doubtfully. "But I just want to get this settled."

"It will be. I have an ace up my sleeve."

"What?"

"I can't tell you. I hope I won't have to use it."

Miss Weston knocked. He said, "Come in," and she told him, "Mrs. Finlay is in the waiting room."

"All right, bring her in." He gave Meg a small loving shove and said, "Keep in touch."

Driving back to the house, Meg thought: If I take Andrew and go away . . .

Where?

She didn't want to go to the Scotts', and she had to work —until she gets me fired, she thought grimly; and even if Clara, amazing Clara, would come with her to look after Andrew, where would they go? She thought of Clara's little house, and couldn't remember if it were rented, or if she had sold it.

When she went into Brand house, she heard voices on

the sunporch and Cornelia called, "Is that you, Meg? Do come on out before you go upstairs."

Apparently, Cornelia had completely recovered from her fatigue. She wore one of her beautifully cut frocks, and her hair had evidently been cosseted by her hairdresser that morning. With her at tea were two middle-aged women, both known to Meg as part of Cornelia's adoring Greek chorus. Andrew had already paid his respects and was back in the nursery; the Misses Reynolds were staying on for dinner.

"And for bridge," said Cornelia gaily. "I do expect you to sacrifice yourself and make a fourth as tomorrow's your day off."

Somehow there's a curious difference between "tomorrow you're off," and "tomorrow's your day off." Meg felt rather like an indulged housemaid.

She refused tea, saying she must shower, change and see Andrew, and Cornelia said casually, "You'll have him on your hands tomorrow. Clara's going to see her mother and also has some business to transact."

Upstairs in the nursery, with Andrew doing his special type of vocalizing, a cross between a hum and a muted howl, Meg said softly, "Nana seems better."

Clara said, "She's fine," and added, "Since you're off tomorrow, I thought I'd better see my mother—I haven't in a couple of weeks—and there are things I want to arrange," she concluded vaguely.

"I'll look after the young master," Meg promised, "although I daresay he'll resent it."

"I'd take him with me," said Clara, "but Mrs. Brand is so afraid he'll catch something." She emitted a refined little snort. "There's nothing in that nursing home *to* catch except old age," she went on. "What with the antibiotics and everything, they're all as safe as incubator babies; safer, I guess. Have you written to your aunt yet, Meg?"

"Yes, and mailed it at the hospital. But I want so much

to talk with her. I thought, after I left the hospital today I'd stop at the hotel, go into the phone booth and get the overseas operator. Then I remembered that she and Ted aren't home; they're in Portugal. He had to go there on business and they won't be back for another week. So I'll just have to wait. Although," she added, "I don't know what I can tell her except what I said in the letter; just that Charles and I are going to be married and if he can manage it, we'll fly to England for a short visit."

Clara said, "Well, even if you can't say what you want to over the phone—and at such prices—at least you'll hear her voice and that will be good for you."

Meg went downstairs in time for drinks, but not before. Dinner was a particular ordeal with the fluttering Reynolds sisters, who looked like twins and weren't; everything about them was in motion, their eyes, their hands, and their narrow pink mouths. They orbited around Cornelia like small, anxious satellites.

Meg had met them shortly after she arrived in Melton and recalled how hastily they had averted their gaze from a pregnancy which was not, at the time, on display. But of course Cornelia had told them. Meg knew that they were distant cousins on the Brand side, living on a small income, in an old house heavily crowded by gloomy trees. She knew also that Cornelia often helped them, provided drives in the country, and an occasional dinner. She also sent Ramsay over with her discarded clothing, always in excellent condition; or with baskets of vegetables and flowers from her garden.

They were two people Cornelia could always count upon, Meg reflected, to fill any embarrassing gap; all she had to do was telephone and send Ramsay over.

Meg had heard her decide aloud, more than once, "I have to have the so and so's here. Necessary but so boring. I think I'll ask the Reynolds girls; poor dears, they get out so seldom."

She used them as if they were temporary fillings in

Time's teeth; they'd do until she managed to insert a good firm inlay.

After dinner, coffee and conversation, mildly spiced with gossip, the Reynolds girls who had long since celebrated—if that's the term—their fiftieth birthdays, seemed to know everyone, if not personally, then by hearsay. After the coffee tray had been removed, they went to the bridge table and cut for partners. Meg was teamed with Cornelia, who played an excellent game. Meg wasn't bad herself, but she had never been overfond of cards; her memory wasn't as tenacious as her partner's, and she played more or less by intuition. The Reynolds team, oddly enough was as good as Cornelia and functioned almost as one entity. Cornelia and Meg lost, but Cornelia was kind about it. She said, "Wool gathering, I think, but we'll forgive you."

The sisters always retired early and Meg was torn between wishing they'd go soon, and that they'd stay until midnight. For once they'd gone, the temporary filling would fall out and she and Cornelia would be back where they'd been last evening.

They left before ten and Cornelia, turning from the door, said, "Would you come into the office for a while, Meg?"

Except in its orderliness, nothing was ever less like an office: an old, beautifully tidy desk, comfortable chairs, and, under a window, plants in a long copper receptacle filled with pebbles.

Cornelia sat down at her desk, motioned Meg to a chair and swung around to face her. She said, "I'm sorry about last night, Meg. I'm afraid I was taken by surprise and reacted accordingly."

There was nothing to say, so Meg was silent. Cornelia went on after a moment. "I've been talking to Amos Perry."

Perry and Perry. The Brand lawyers in Melton, Meg thought, as Cornelia went on smoothly. "I've never told you this because there was no reason why I should. But the will I made shortly after Andrew was born also affects you."

"How?" asked Meg.

"I have left you," said Cornelia, sitting erect, her fine ankles crossed, "a trust fund which will yield a comfortable income. Eventually it will return to Andrew. There were no strings to it. I had, of course, considered that you might remarry, but this would not alter the conditions. However, I'm seeing Amos tomorrow and will make one slight change: If, during my lifetime, you marry someone of whom I cannot approve, the trust fund goes into the estate."

Meg said angrily, "It would be simpler if you just took me out of your will altogether."

"I can, of course."

"I'm not interested in a trust fund; I'm not interested in your will," said Meg. "Charles can provide for Andrew and me."

"Are you suggesting that I change my will entirely and leave Andrew out?"

"No, I think that, when the time comes, Andy's son should be entitled to his own personal security. Until then Charles will be responsible for him."

"And should anything happen to Charles?"

"I can work," said Meg. Then, after a brief silence, "Blackmail does not become you, Nana."

Cornelia flushed slightly. She said, "That's an ill-considered word and—insulting."

"But it fits," Meg told her.

Cornelia said, "There's nothing to be gained by this rather offensive sparring. It was natural for me to provide for my son's widow as well as his child."

"And to dictate whom I could or could not marry?"

"It's been done before," said Cornelia. "Now if it had been Dr. Lansing . . ."

Meg's color was high, "Keith Lansing has nothing to do with this."

"Perhaps, indirectly. Have you told Charles about your relationship with him?"

The brilliant color receded. She asked incredulously, "What are you trying to say?"

"I'm not trying to say anything. I've already said it."

"No relationship, as you call it, ever existed between me and Keith," Meg said.

"Is that what you told Andy?"

"Andy?" Her eyes widened. "But there was nothing to tell."

"My dear child," said Cornelia, as if amused. "I suppose you would think it nothing. Are you so"—she hesitated a moment—"innocent, perhaps, that you didn't realize that I would have your entire background looked into, as soon as I returned home from my trip?"

"Just what do you mean, 'looked into'?"

Cornelia said, "I employ lawyers in Boston, as well as the firm here. They've handled several matters for me; they are discreet. They have also, from time to time, employed for their various clients equally discreet private investigators. I had intended to see them in Boston, but talked to the older partner by telephone from the Cape. The facts relative to you which they have held for me were mailed. They are now in the little wall safe."

"Exactly what facts?"

"The background," said Cornelia, "is quite admirable—your parents, your aunt, your scholastic records, and your hospital training. However, at the time you were doing post graduate work you saw Dr. Lansing frequently."

Meg said furiously, "You had no right!"

"Every right. Did you think my son could marry a girl entirely unknown to me and I not be—anxious?"

Meg said suddenly, "I remember now. I did tell Andy about Keith."

"Oh," said Cornelia and her regard sharpened. "And what did you tell him?"

Now she was remembering fully, the golden beach, the sea and Andy asking her, "How about lovers?"

She said steadily, "When we were in Greece, Andy asked me if I'd had lovers. I told him one—almost. I said, I was the marrying kind and that he—meaning Keith—wasn't. I also said there was a certain amount of temptation. And that's all we ever said about it."

Cornelia said, "But he's not here to testify to that, you know. It appears there were two young women with whom you shared an apartment. One of them was killed in an automobile accident shortly after you went to England."

Meg said, "I know," and remembered the shock she had suffered when she heard about Lily—pretty and happy, a kind, friendly girl with tremendous vitality.

"The other one," Cornelia went on, "completed her studies after you were married and went as an instructor to the hospital in which you both trained."

That one was Susie. Meg had heard from her at the time Lily was killed, not since. Susie was the plain one, a plodder. Meg remembered that it was through Susie that Keith had first come to the apartment.

Cornelia said, "She—her name escapes me—was more than willing to talk about you. She kept a journal, so she even supplied dates."

"Susie would. I daresay she said that Keith came to see me when neither she nor Lily were in the apartment?"

"Yes."

"You're incredible," Meg said flatly.

Cornelia said blandly, "Perhaps. At any rate most people do tend to jump to conclusions."

"Andy didn't."

Cornelia said astonishingly, "I doubt whether Andy would have cared, Meg. He was, I'm sorry to say, uninterested in the disciplines and conventions of the older generation. Charles, however," she added thoughtfully, "whether you know it or not, is extremely conventional; and with good reason."

Meg said, with contempt, "Charles may be conventional,

as you say—I haven't found him so—but he isn't stupid and also, he loves me. Even if you had a dozen private investigators bribing Susie—and I've no doubt they did—nothing you can say will make the slightest difference to him."

"Perhaps not, but what if Dr. Lansing were to be consulted?"

Meg laughed. She said, "Keith Lansing is married, has two children, and his wife is pregnant. I hardly think he would endanger his comfortable life and his marriage. It wouldn't be to his interest to lie about me and himself."

Cornelia smiled, "I talked with him, you know, when he was here and alone. His comfortable life as you put it is endangered. His wife intends to leave him after the child is born. She's returning to her parents. Despite his seeming lack of worry about funds, he'll have to find further financing for his hospital."

"I don't believe his wife is leaving him——"

"Oh, but she is. It seems that her parents don't approve of his interest in other women; nor does his wife. She's been conveniently pregnant three times now. She was strongly urged to leave him after the first child was born, but didn't."

"He can't have told you all this!"

"He didn't," Cornelia admitted. "Not all, that is, and I do advise you to think things over before you decide to marry Charles Scott and take Andrew from me. Helen Scott tried to take my husband. You've wondered why my friendship with the Scotts ceased. That is why. She was here in my house one night. Bill Scott was away. She was drunk. I asked my husband to drive her home because she refused to stay here overnight. There was no one in the Scott house but Sarah, and she was on the third floor, asleep."

Cornelia was ashen, she shook, and Meg felt a sudden compassion for her. She said, "Please don't go on, Nana."

Cornelia said dully, "He'd been drinking too, if not as much. He came home hours later and told me . . . he sat on the edge of our bed and cried. We went away the next day on a trip. When we came back, Helen openly pursued him. I went to William Scott. That's what happened."

Meg said, "But all this has nothing to do with Charles and me, Nana."

Cornelia's eyes glittered. She said, "Andy's father was a very handsome man; he was also, weak. He regretted this—episode—to the end of his life. Sometimes I think it killed him. I've never forgiven Helen Scott, I never shall."

Meg said, "But you said she was drunk——"

"Oh, yes," said Cornelia, "she was drunk, but not so drunk that she didn't know what she was doing. I didn't see her. Bill Scott wouldn't permit it. He heard what I had to say and told me to get out of his house. He was always a fool about her."

She rose. She said, "I'm going upstairs. I don't care what you do. You can call Charles; you can do anything you please. But if you marry him, I'll find some way to keep Andrew."

Thirteen

MEG, WATCHING CORNELIA leave the room without haste, felt like a small animal, freezing under the glare of headlights or at a hostile sound, statue still; she was experiencing the panic of a trapped creature.

After a few minutes she rose with an effort, went to Cornelia's desk and opened the telephone book. She'd called the Scott house only once, and couldn't remember the number. She found, and dialed it. Her hearing seemed to have sharpened, as an animal's does, she thought she heard Cornelia moving about upstairs; she believed people were whispering in the kitchen and the ringing of the Scotts' bell seemed unnaturally loud.

Helen Scott answered. She has such a quiet voice, Meg thought and her eyes filled. Helen knew something about traps.

"Yes?"

"This is Meg Brand, Mrs. Scott. I hate to disturb you at this hour——"

"It's not late. I always look at the news. I'm up in my bedroom. Bill's out. Do you want to speak to Charles?"

"Is he there?" She found herself gasping, her free hand at her throat.

"He came in a little while ago. I'll call him." Then her voice changed. It was as if she were aware of the panic, there in Cornelia's office. She said sharply, "Don't hang up."

A minute, two minutes went by, slower than a century passes. During it, Meg started to replace the transmitter but didn't.

Eventually, "Darling," he said, "what's wrong?"

"I don't know. I'm scared. I thought if I could just hear you speak . . ."

She wanted to cry, she wanted to say, "I'm here in this house with a madwoman . . . or maybe I'm crazy . . ."

"Simmer down. Take a deep breath." He also knew panic when he heard it, as he had many times, and from many people, ill and well. "I'll come at once."

"Please," she said forlornly. "But don't come to the house, Charles, I'll walk down the driveway and meet you at the stone wall, by the entrance."

"Okay. The wind's freshened; put on a coat; tie a scarf over your head. We can talk in the car. I'll be there in fifteen minutes."

Meg hung up, left the cell, with its imprisoning walls and went upstairs. When she appeared without knocking, in Clara's room, Clara, reading in bed, her radio playing softly, was startled. "What's the matter? Are you ill?" she asked.

"No," Meg told her. Her eyes blazed, her hair seemed to blaze also; she was like a wavering flame. She said, "I'm going to meet Charles at the driveway entrance. I wanted you to know where I'd be."

"It's so late——" Clara began.

"I know. I have to see him, Clara. I don't know what to do," and Clara thought: I've read about people wringing their hands, but I never saw anyone do it till now.

She said gently, "All right. Take it easy. I'll be awake when you come back."

"We'll sit in his car," said Meg. She added, "This can't wait until tomorrow, Clara."

She went from the room and closed the door, not softly, uncaring. Clara leaned back against her pillows, her thin gray braids over her spare shoulders, and thought irrelevantly that she'd forgotten to pin them up, under a net. Then she thought: Damn her; but she was not thinking of Meg.

Meg went downstairs and took her coat and a scarf from the closet. She left the door on the latch so she could get in without ringing, and turned on the outside lights which Morton had switched off when the Reynolds women left. She walked down the driveway. She'd have to wait outside, but it was infinitely preferable to remaining in the house. At the end of the driveway, the gate posts and a stone wall curved away on either side. She went past the posts and sat on the wall, on the left. She was cold, huddled in her coat, but not because of the September night and the slight chill in the wind. She looked at dark trees, she heard them speaking, she looked at a dark sky sequined with stars, bright and indifferent. She listened, hearing something scuttle in the bushes, hearing cars long before they passed, praying childishly: Let it be the next one.

When Charles came, driving fast, squealing around the curves and corners, he saw her in his headlights, sitting on the wall, waiting. He stopped the car, got out and came to the wall. He said, "Let's sit in the car."

She felt as if she were part of the cold stone; she could not move. She shook her head and the scarf fell off.

Charles reached up and lifted her down into his arms and held her. He said, "It's all right, Meg, I'm here."

She began to laugh, "Bedside or wallside manner?" she asked.

"No hysterics." He held her close. "Come on, get in the car and tell me what happened. Mom was very disturbed; she all but threw me out of the house; she kept saying, 'Hurry!' You could have come to us, you know."

They'd reached the car, and he put her in it. She said huskily, "I was afraid to drive. For the first time since I learned how, I was afraid, and scared to leave Andrew even with Clara."

"All right, take another deep breath. You'll stop shaking. Talk to me," he said. "Be a good girl, this isn't going to hurt, not really."

She was a child in a doctor's office. The foolish, tender admonition and reassurance steadied her. She said obediently, "Nana had the Reynolds sisters from teatime through dinner and then bridge. They left about ten and she asked me into her office."

"Go on." She thought: I would rather die than tell him what she said about his mother.

She told him everything but that, sometimes her words stumbled, sometimes she cried and he waited, holding her. She told him about Keith Lansing and about the private investigators.

Charles could be fluently profane. He was now. He said pleasantly, "Look, honey, why do you always press the panic button? I keep telling you there is no way, none at all, by which she can prevent your marriage or take Andrew from you."

"She could go into court," Meg said, "and say I'm unfit to bring up a child."

"Well you're not," he said calmly, "nor am I. And no judge would believe that little yarn of hers, not even if your former friend swears by the book that she was stationed under the bed on numerous occasions. It's absurd. Also, courts don't separate a young child from his mother unless she has a history of promiscuity, drugs, drinking——"

"It wouldn't just be Susie, it could be Keith too."

"Oh that bastard," he said casually. "A small-time, two timing, synthetic Casanova. Record as long as your arm, but those of us who knew him in the Navy can testify he was more often frustrated than not. Not every girl fell for the charm. Poor Francesca."

"If what Nana said is true, Francesca is going to divorce him, and he'll need money for the hospital. . . ."

"I wish you'd stop calling Cornelia Brand that vomitous name."

"Cornelia, then. Suppose she offers to help? I know the plans have been made, he talked about them when he was here; the land has been bought; the architects and builders hired. His wife's people will certainly cut off that source, and if any of the Wainwrights' friends pledged money, they'll withdraw; they'll be on the Wainwrights' side. Suppose Cornelia offers to help? She can afford it. He'd have nothing to lose."

"Except his reputation, such as it is. People—some of them—still make faces when a doctor is divorced by his wife; not as many as used to, of course. But if he tampers with ancient history, to his own detriment, that's something else again. Besides, I don't think he'd do it, Meg—he isn't that tough; and he has kids. If he expects to make another good marriage. . . . Oh, that reminds me—you'd be in the running if Cornelia gets rid of me."

"Oh, shut up," said Meg exasperated. "I'm sorry to be such an idiot."

"You should be. Talk about molehills! Now, I'm taking you back to the house. I've brought you some sleeping pills."

"But I never——"

"You're off tomorrow, aren't you?"

"Yes."

"Then take them. . . . What are your plans?"

"Clara's going out, Cornelia is seeing her lawyers. She intends to cut me out of her will," she said, and found herself laughing.

"Good grief!" said Charles. "Here and now, consider our engagement broken. . . . What else?"

"I'll be taking care of Andrew."

"Okay. So bring him to the house, introduce him to his future step-grandparents and Sarah; Dad will be around. I'll look in when I can. . . . Now it's your turn to shut up."

He kissed her; the tension flowed out of her, and she clung to him. The shaking had stopped. She said, "Of course I'm a fool. I don't know how you stand me."

"Sheer willpower."

"But when anything threatens Andrew," she said, "however far-fetched . . ." She began to shiver again. She said, "I told you she was out of her mind."

"Put her out of yours. You'll have Andrew and you'll have me."

"But he's so little," she said desolately, "and so attached to her. She's the most exciting thing in his life."

"We'll keep him stirred up," said Charles firmly. "And Mom and Dad will spoil him something horrible. Now, back to Wuthering Heights. Here." He put a small envelope in her hand. "Take two of these. You'll sleep."

He started the car, turned in between the gate posts, drove in, and stopped. Brakes shrieked, bluestone scattered. He got out, opened the door and gave her his hand. He said, raising his voice somewhat, "Good night darling. Sleep well, and don't worry. All systems point to Go."

He took her to the house and kissed her again, standing under the outdoor lights, smiling.

She heard him drive away. There was not a sound in the house. She locked up, switched off the lights, and went upstairs.

Clara's light was still on. Meg knocked and entered.

"Where's your scarf?"

"I must have dropped it. I'm all right now, Clara."

"Want me to fix you some hot milk, with or without bourbon?"

"No. I have some sleeping pills. Charles gave them to me."

"You look better. Feel it?"

"Yes," said Meg. "Good night, dear."

Meg closed Clara's door and a moment later her own. Whether Cornelia was awake, whether she slept and the

165

sounds woke her, she didn't know and couldn't have cared less. After she was ready for bed, she came out of the bathroom, took a thermos from the bedside table which Morton kept filled and poured a glass of water. She shook two capsules into her hand, swallowed them, got into bed, and turned out the light.

It had been some time since dinner; she had eaten very little. She felt empty, as if drained. She ached, as if bruised. The sleeping pills acted within a very short time. Drowsiness crept over her like a quiet, inexorable fog and then she was part of the fog, drifting without memory, thought, or sound into sleep.

Someone knocked at her door, once, and then again, sharply, and Meg opened her eyes. For a moment she remembered nothing. The sun streamed in and the curtains stirred in the wind.

"Who is it?" she asked sleepily.

"Just me." Clara came in. She asked anxiously, "You all right?"

"I'm fine. I took the pills . . . it was heavenly just to sleep. Like falling into a dark cave but not hurting myself. What time is it, Clara?"

"After ten."

"Good lord." Meg sat up. "I'm sorry. I'll get dressed right away. I know you're going out."

"Not yet. Mrs. Brand has already gone, she left word she wouldn't be back for lunch. Pull yourself together and I'll bring you some coffee. Andrew's in the kitchen with the Mortons."

Meg said, "You know I think I have a hangover."

"Probably coffee will fix it. I'll be right back. Why don't I ask Mrs. Morton to pack you a lunch? You can take Andrew on a picnic. It's a wonderful day."

Meg said, "Andrew and I have never been on a picnic

alone. But we'll both wish you were with us, Clara; and last night Charles asked me to bring Andrew to his house to see his mother and Sarah."

"Well," said Clara, after a moment, "it's your child and your decision. Get up, Meg; I'll be back in a few minutes with the coffee." She watched Meg swing her long legs over the side of the bed. She said, "Like as not you'll feel dizzy. . . . The Mortons will keep Andrew occupied for a while."

Meg felt dizzy enough; her head ached slightly; the fog that some hours ago had been beneficent sleep was now in her brain. She shook her head to clear it. A shower, warm, then cool; the daily ritual of brushing her teeth and washing her face. She remembered what her friend Judy had once said to her while they were in training: "The trouble with life is it's so daily." Yes, of course, but only on the surface. Beneath that surface, smooth as her own young skin, the fears, earthquakes, upheavals, and uncertainty.

She went back to her room, put on a bed jacket, got into bed, folded her hands primly, and waited.

Clara came in with a tray: coffee, lots of it, in a silver pot, juice, dry toast, butter on an ironstone pat, and another one of bitter marmalade.

She drank the first cup under Clara's watchful eye, put a little of the marmalade on a wedge of toast and said, "Reminds me of England."

"Thought it would," said Clara. "Get dressed, when you've finished. I'll get Andrew ready. He's running around like a chicken with its head off, and Mrs. Morton is packing lunch."

Clara had a little old car. Later she took off in it, wearing a longish dark dress, a hat with daisies on it perched on her head. She also wore gloves and carried an enormous handbag. She said, as Meg and Andrew waved from the driveway, "Take care. Have fun. I'll see you, before teatime."

Andrew regarded the car gravely as it went sedately down

the drive. He stood with his fat sturdy legs apart, hampered by the rubber pants, and looked up at his mother. His sunny baby face grew old and a little frightened. He asked, "Clara going away?"

"She'll be back, darling. Now, you and I are going on a picnic."

"Nana?" asked Andrew, still bewildered.

"She'll be back too," said Meg. "Come on in the house, and get ready for our picnic."

"Picnic," he shouted, a baby again, seeing only the moment, the immediate present, uninterested in the future, casting the past behind him as one disposes of a soiled tissue.

Presently they were in her car . . . or, as she'd come to think of it, Cornelia's, with Andrew securely belted in and the picnic hamper on the back seat. She drove about for a while, showing him the objects he could see from the window. He tried to stand up; it was safe enough, so she let him. He saw cows, and horses, a big dog running, and bright birds flying. He saw the ruffled surface of a lake, like an old mirror; and the winding of a small river. This was, his mother realized, his first very personal outing. His many rides with Cornelia, tucked under her arm, with Ramsay cautiously in the driver's seat, had been different. Cornelia, who thought a great deal about externals, had never bothered to point out a few of them to Andrew. Now he was a part of everything he saw: the winding roads, the high sailing clouds, the sunlight, the ineffable blue of the sky, the bending and whispering of the trees, and of the wind.

Eventually, they came to the place which Meg had selected, a picnic ground; not Scenic Rest, forbidden by Cornelia and the Garden Club, but beyond that on a side road; a public place, open and sunny, but with shade trees, tables, benches, fireplaces, and a little brook.

There were others there; two families complete with children; and tucked away among the trees a convenience to which Meg conducted her son. He was entranced. "No chain," he announced.

Back at the table where she'd left the small hamper, Andrew in a frenzy of freedom was running about, making friends with the youngsters older than himself, and regarded indulgently by their parents. "What a darling little boy," said one woman, leading Andrew back by his hand.

He also fell in love with a couple of dogs, which may or may not have belonged to the other picnickers. Cornelia had no dogs. She did not like them, or cats.

In the hamper, lovingly packed by Mrs. Morton, there were chicken sandwiches, fruit, love apples, and celery; there were also cookies and things to drink; for Andrew, milk, cold from the thermos; for Meg, iced tea.

She had been alone with Andrew before on rare occasions when Clara left the house and Cornelia was out, but not as alone as this, not even when she had carried him from conception to delivery.

When the picnic was over, she said, "Now we must pack up." She indicated the wastebaskets and put the paper napkins and the rest of the throwaways in his small hands, "Think you can put these in the basket?" she asked, and Andrew nodded, his face grave with responsibility.

"Then do it," she said, laughing, "and come back for the paper cups."

When he had done so, he climbed into her lap, and yawned. His eyelids fell, the innocent eyelids of childhood. His face was a little flushed. Nothing was written on it but youth and trust and inexperience.

Sitting on the hard backless bench, Meg rocked him in her arms. "Take a nap," she told him, "just a little nap."

The excitement, the sun, the wind, the running free had made him sleepy. He said drowsily, "Doggie," but the black and white mixed breed which had been nosing about them, had gone. There was nothing more to feed him. The other families were packing up; they were leaving, in their station wagons. They were waving good-by.

After a while Meg carried Andrew to the car. He was sleeping soundly as only a child sleeps. She put him on the back seat and got in with him, looking out at the serene September day. It was a dream; she did not wish to awaken from it.

When Andrew woke, all of one piece, coming to life with a bounce, his eyes wide, she ruffled the red-gold hair and said, "I'm here. Now, we're going to see someone."

"See someone," he repeated.

"Yes . . . Charles's mother. She corrected herself. "Uncle Charles," she said.

"Charles," said Andrew firmly.

"Bathroom?"

Andrew shook his head. He then felt his small rear end, and reported, "All dry."

So she drove away from that serene and sunlit place and went toward town and the Scott house, Andrew strapped beside her in the front seat, looking out of the window. She was astonished at how many landmarks he recognized. The church; he pointed to the soaring white spire. The cemetery, but he turned away from that. A drugstore. He said tentatively, "Ice cream?" But she shook her head. "Enough's enough," she told him.

And so by easy stages, they came to the big house on the hill, with its shabby porch and uneven steps. As Meg stopped the car, Helen Scott was there, in a tweed skirt and a pullover; Sarah behind her, and, looming in the doorway, the elder Dr. Scott.

He came down the steps and opened the car door. He said, "Hello" to Meg and "Hi" to Andrew. He did not demean him by chin chucking. He simply unbuckled him, lifted him out, and smote him on the bottom. "Up the steps," he ordered.

Andrew was careful. He hadn't forgotten falling. There was no gate here. He reached for the railing. It was too high, so he held fast to the posts, and when Meg would have gone to help him, Bill Scott said, "Let him go; he won't fall far and we're here."

Very like his Charles, she thought.

Helen Scott, watching from the porch, smiled. She did not hold out her arms. She knew better than that. She waited quietly, and Andrew, achieving the porch level, staggered toward her and flung his arms about her knees. She said then, "Hello, Andy."

Meg, walking up the steps with Bill Scott, suiting pace to his, looked up startled. Andrew looked up too, scowling a little, and Helen said to Meg, "You don't call him Andy?"

"No, I—I was going to, but his grandmother didn't like it."

"I see."

"He looks like Andy. I remember Andy at his age," said Helen, her hand on the small, round head.

Now, it was Sarah's turn. She said briskly, "High time I met you." She held out her hand, and Andrew put his in it; she shook it gravely.

"Come on in the house," said Helen, leading the way, "I think Charles will stop by. He's at the office and going on to the hospital."

"Charles?" said Andrew and looked around for him.

"He'll be here soon," said Helen. "What have you been doing," she hesitated and then said—"Andrew?" For a moment her gray eyes clouded.

"Picnic," said Andrew happily.

"Good for you," said Sarah. "Want to come with me? We have a puppy and baby chicks outside."

She took him away and Meg sat with Charles's parents in the big cool room. The shades were drawn against the sun. She leaned back against her chair and closed her eyes. Her head still ached. Then she spoke, carefully, as if forcing herself.

"I'm so sorry about last night," she said.

Bill Scott grunted. He was nursing a cold pipe. He wasn't supposed to smoke, but sometimes he did. Mostly, however, he went about with the stem clamped between his teeth and no tobacco in the bowl. He said, "Helen told me."

"I—I was a little hysterical."

He asked after a moment, "Cornelia give you a rough time?"

Meg said after a moment, "I thought so. Perhaps I only imagined it."

"I don't think you're given to flights of fancy," said Dr. Scott.

She said, faltering, "You're very kind to me."

"That be damned," said Charles's father. "You belong to us now," and Helen said, in her quiet voice, "We'd like to have you think so, once you're used to the idea."

A car drove in, and stopped; there were hurried footsteps on the porch and Charles barreled in. He went over to Meg, put his hand on her hair, and asked, "Get some sleep?"

"Too much. I had a hangover this morning."

"I expected you would. Where's your infant?"

"He's out with Sarah."

Charles said, sitting down, "Well we're glad to have you both aboard."

He produced a small unmalicious anecdote relative to Mrs. Elgin and the hospital and told it, at great length. Sarah appeared with Andrew and asked, "Can he have ice cream, Mrs. Brand? I've some in the freezer."

Meg said he could, so Andrew went off to sit at the kitchen table with a dish of ice cream before him, a napkin around his neck, and Sarah beaming at him, remembering his father's invasions of her kitchen.

"Council of war?" suggested Dr. Scott and Meg looked at Charles. "Did you tell them?" she asked.

"Not yet; not without your permission."

She said, and sighed, "I—I'd almost forgotten and your parents will think me a complete idiot."

Helen said, "I doubt if you'll ever manage to say Mother and Father. Perhaps, later, Mom and Dad? I hope so. Try now, for Helen and Bill."

Meg looked at her gratefully. She said, "I'd rather Charles told you."

He did so, undramatically. He said, "It's hearsay, of course, because unfortunately I wasn't there. But this is briefly what Meg reported last night."

They listened in silence until Charles had finished and then Dr. Scott said reflectively, "Cornelia was always a bitch."

"Bill," said his wife. Her color rose, but she looked at him with love. She said, "She can't help it, you know, poor woman."

Dr. Scott went over and sat on the arm of his wife's chair. He said, "Don't be too good to be true, Helen."

Charles said, "This gets us nowhere; questioning Aunt Cornelia's ancestry is beyond the point. Besides it insults a lot of good bitches I've known, the four-legged variety."

Meg said faintly, "What am I going to do, Doctor—I mean, Bill?"

"Nothing," said Charles's father promptly. "If she talks, listen. Don't argue with her. All that will come later, if at all. When do you kids want to be married?"

Charles said, "I've been asking around. Prescott will take over for me. . . . I thought, the end of next month."

Bill Scott laughed. He said. "It's not in character for Cornelia to give you a fashionable wedding, Meg; on the other hand, she dislikes town gossip. I suggest church, just ourselves, and Cornelia if she condescends, and I daresay she will; it will save face. Still thinking of going to England?"

Charles said, "Of course," and Meg said, "I do want to—and Clara, I think, will go with us."

"Cornelia will take it hard," said Scott. "It will be like losing her right arm and her left leg. Has Clara spoken to her?"

"Not yet, nothing's settled . . . I just hoped."

Charles said, "Stop worrying. Take it a day at a time. Murder may be in Auntie's heart, but I doubt if she'd stoop to physical violence."

His mother said warningly, "I hear Sarah and Andrew coming." She rose, as Meg did, and put her arms around the younger woman. She said, "It will all come out right. You'll see."

Meg said, feeling the warmth of the slender arms around her, "I know. Only it's been so"—she looked for a word, and found it—"degrading."

"Yes," said Helen steadily. "But, remember, we're here. Pick up a phone, get in a car."

Charles said, "One for all." He smiled, but his eyes did not. "Hi, Andrew," he said, as Andrew catapulted into the room and Sarah said sedately, "He had his dish of ice cream. I washed his face and hands and took him to the bathroom. He seems to like the privy at the picnic place better. He told me so."

"He said, 'no chain' when he was there." Meg shook her head, she added, "But the only place he has seen a chain is off the Brand kitchen. It must have impressed him."

Andrew didn't want to go home. Meg bribed him, saying, "Clara will be waiting for us."

"And Nana?" he inquired.

"Nana, too," said Meg, her heart heavier than it was a moment before.

Helen kissed her good-by; she did not venture to kiss Andrew, but he offered her his cheek; and, to Sarah. Dr. Scott shook hands with him and Charles whacked his little shoulder. Then he put them in their car, leaned in and kissed Meg. Andrew contemplated this with some astonishment but without disapproval. "See you tomorrow," said Charles, "at the hospital. Meantime if the volcano erupts, call out the troops."

They drove away, smiling a little. She felt that she and Andrew had been in a very safe place and that it would always be there for them both.

Fourteen

C LARA WAS WAITING for them outside as they reached the house. Meg unstrapped her restless son and he scrambled out and into Clara's arms. You would have thought they'd been parted for years, Meg reflected, putting the car in the garage, and walking back slowly.

What would she and Andrew do if Clara didn't come with them, if Cornelia refused to let her go? But she can't, Meg assured herself. Clara's a grown woman.

When she went in, Clara was alone in the hall. She said, "Andrew's upstairs with his grandmother." She smiled briefly at Meg. "I don't have to ask either of you if you had a good time. I thought maybe Mrs. Brand would pass up the romp this evening. She was here when I came back, in her office with the door shut. Later she rang for Morton and said she'd have dinner in her room."

"Is she ill?"

"Headache," Clara said. She paused. "Seems she's been having more of those than usual. I suggested calling Doctor Foster, but she wouldn't hear of it. Said she had medicine; that it had been another tiring day. I also suggested that Andrew just run in and say good night, but she vetoed that too."

Meg said, "Andrew may not be able yet to carry on a detailed conversation, but I bet he'll be able to tell her where and with whom he's been. I was going to tell her when I saw her." She added, "Her headache will be worse by now. . . . How was your day, Clara?"

"All right. . . . I'll go fetch Andrew for his bath and we'll have supper with him downstairs."

"Probably an anticlimax for him. Sarah gave him the run of her kitchen, Dr. and Mrs. Scott charmed him almost as much as the chickens and the new puppy Sarah took him out to see. He wasn't afraid. He fell on the puppy and rolled with him; good thing he didn't with the chickens. I'm afraid he won't eat much, Clara; he did full justice to Mrs. Morton's picnic lunch—I must go tell her how good it was—and also Sarah gave him ice cream."

When Meg returned from the kitchen and Mrs. Morton, Clara was at the foot of the stairs. She said, "I'm to tell Morton to bring Andrew's little table and chair from the nursery. He's to have supper with his grandmother, early. I'll go back and give him his bath now."

Later, in her room, Meg heard sounds of hilarity from Cornelia's quarters and when she heard Clara go in, opened her door.

"Good night darling," said Cornelia, "sleep tight."

" 'Night," said Andrew.

Cornelia's door closed. Meg went into the hall and picked Andrew up. He's getting heavy, she thought; and he's going to be as tall as his father, taller maybe. He was clutching Bunny and she looked inquiringly at Clara. "He insisted, and got permission," Clara explained.

After Andrew was in bed, Meg knocked at Cornelia's door and when Cornelia asked, "Clara?" she said, "No, it's Meg. May I come in?"

"Do," said Cornelia politely. She was sitting up in bed, the little table and chair and the supper trays had been taken away. A book lay face down beside her. She put aside her reading glasses and said agreeably, "Andrew told me about your outing."

"He likes picnics," Meg said from the foot of the bed. "Mrs. Morton packed a hamper. We both enjoyed it."

"Where did you go?"

Meg told her and Cornelia's eyebrows lifted . . . "Oh, the public place," she commented. "You could have picnicked right here; that's why we have a table and benches by the brook."

"We drove around first," Meg explained.

"And afterwards to the Scotts."

"That's right. When Charles knew I'd have Andrew for the day, he asked me to bring him to the house."

"Thoughtful of him." Cornelia's lightly rouged mouth drew back from her excellent teeth. "So you went, although you knew it was the last place I'd wish Andrew to go?" she asked.

"Yes."

Cornelia shrugged her shoulders under the rosy bed jacket. She inquired, "What did you want to see me about?"

"Clara told me you had a bad headache. I thought perhaps I could do something for you."

"You've done quite enough," said Cornelia evenly. "Good night, Meg."

"Good night," Meg said and escaped gratefully; cold and hot by turns. She thought: Why am I so terrified of her? I wasn't at first—just strange and a little scared. But she was Andy's mother, she offered us a home, and Andy wanted us here. But now . . . I keep telling myself that she's powerless really. Threatening to cut me, or even Andrew, out of her will is empty and meaningless. Why, when I stood and looked at her just now was I half paralyzed with fear? I've never been neurotic, never.

At dinner.

"Was Andrew upset or overtired?" Meg asked. "I didn't think so, but——"

"Did Mrs. Brand say so?" Clara interrupted.

"No."

"He wasn't. Does him good to get out, see people, not just at teatime on parade for company. He had a ball. He's been talking six to the dozen. What did Sarah think of him?"

"She didn't say, but I assume favorably."

Clara laughed. She said, "Sarah was crazy about Andy. He was in and out of that house so often, as much at home as Charles." She was silent a moment, and then went on, "The renters in my house—it is mine, my mother signed it over to me—want to buy it. I saw them today; they offered a good price."

"Are you going to sell?"

"That depends. I'm thinking about it." She looked at Meg steadily. She said, "I've got a special use for the money —two uses, really. I have to think about old age; I'd be better off renting, or perhaps buying a little apartment in town."

"Clara if you come with us   "

"I'll still have to retire someday and I'll still want a place to go to on my days off. . . . I expect you'd give me days off? I've missed having no place to go except to friends and the nursing home ever since Mama gave up the cottage."

"You've told me only one use for the money."

"The other—well, that's so I could be free to be with you and Andrew." She added, "I owe Mrs. Brand a lot."

"Oh, Clara," said Meg. "We can help, Charles and I."

"No. This is just between me and Mrs. Brand." She added, "I planned to leave whatever little I might have left when I died to Andrew. Maybe there'll still be something, I don't know. In a way, I'm leaving it to him," she said thoughtfully, "while I'm alive."

Morton came in, to clear and then to bring dessert, so they talked from then on only of the picnic and the drive. "Andrew recognized a lot of things," said Meg.

"He's not stupid," Clara said reprovingly.

When they'd had coffee, Clara went upstairs and Meg said, "I'll be up later. I'm going for a walk."

Passing the hall table she saw letters on it; she'd forgotten all about mail; perhaps there was something for her and it had slipped Morton's mind, or Cornelia's.

Idly turning over the envelopes, she found only a postal airmailed from Portugal, under the outgoing mail, usually left there for Ramsay to pick up. The letter on the top was addressed in Cornelia's square, black handwriting—she hated typewriters—to Dr. Keith Lansing. Meg could not help seeing it, and she had the distinct impression that Cornelia had intended her to do so. It was evidently to reach him at his office, and was marked "Personal."

Meg got her coat, put the postcard in her pocket and went out. She thought: I may as well look for my scarf.

She found it, blown against the stone wall and caught there by a projection. She freed it, tied it about her hair, sat once more on the wall and found herself listening for cars. She thought: Why would she write Keith?

Cornelia, if she had anything serious to say to Dr. Lansing, would not put it in writing. She was not a fool. If she had something to offer him for value received now or in the future, she wouldn't say so; she'd suggest that if he were to come this way . . . or that she might be in his city and, if so, would like to see him.

I should have read it. . . . No, I should have torn it up, Meg thought savagely. But that could have been stupidity. You just don't read another person's mail.

She had a clear vision of Cornelia and Keith sitting on the terrace, or alone in the living room, or facing each other across his desk in another city. But what could she say? Would she spell it out? You're going to be divorced; your plans for the hospital will suffer. I'm in a position to help you quite anonymously of course. And if he asked why, she'd tell him. All she'd want was the assurance that if, in her turn, she needed help, he'd provide it.

But Charles was right; Keith couldn't afford one scandal on top of another. He wouldn't dare lend himself to it, not for all the money in the world. He was a clever, charming, practical man; there were better ways to get money. Maybe the Wainwrights and their friends wouldn't give what they'd pledged, but there were other people; and there were reputable doctors who'd be more than willing to make an investment. All Keith would have to sacrifice would be some of his authority, and that just for a while, since physicians and surgeons with the money to invest would probably be older than himself.

All Cornelia was doing was turning over stones to see what might profitably crawl out from under them.

After a while Meg went back to the house; she gave the hall table a wide berth as if something revolting lay upon it. In her own room she read the postcard from her aunt. It said, "More to follow. Very excited about your letter. It's heavenly here. Wish you and Andrew were with us." She thought: She doesn't say when they'll be home; she never did give me the date. I'll telephone from town at the end of next week.

She saw Charles briefly at the hospital the next day. He asked, coming into her office, "Busy?"

"Naturally. What can I do for you, Doctor?"

"Nothing, here. I just wanted to say that the future step-grandparents are enchanted by your offspring; Sarah too, and Tiger."

"Tiger?"

"The puppy. He hasn't stopped howling since Andrew left." He looked at her carefully. "How did Aunt Cornelia take your—escapade. I imagine you told her."

"I'd intended to, but Andrew beat me to it. She was not amused."

"The Queen's been dead for some time," he remarked. "No, I daresay neither amused nor pleased. Look, I've got things pretty well in hand now. . . . Dad says firmly he'll see patients at the office, his old ones. They'll be delighted. He'll have to get permission though. I don't think it will hurt him; he's getting stir crazy and besides he hates being cautious; he's always worked without a net."

Meg laughed. "That's what Andy used to say about himself."

"Yes, I know. Anyway, Prescott will take the house calls and the hospital, and a little getting back into a loose harness will be good for Dad. . . . How about dinner, the three of us, soon? We'll put our heads together and make plans."

"Clara's making plans too, to sell her house and to come with us. She told me so."

"But she needn't sell it——" he began.

"She feels she must repay Cornelia whatever she's spent—at the nursing home."

Charles whistled. "I hadn't thought of that—why, I don't know—but it's exactly like Clara."

"I've been thinking—perhaps we shouldn't let her do it."

"It's her affair," said Charles. "She won't be the first person to buy freedom."

"Suppose Cornelia refuses?"

"Well, Clara will have offered, won't she? That's all that's necessary. I had a little talk with Clara incidentally, that Tuesday before you came home, before dinner and the eruption of the proper Bostonians along with their hospitable cousin. Not that Jean has ever been particularly proper."

"Is Clara the ace up your sleeve?"

"No."

Mrs. Elgin came in from her office. Charles rose and said courteously, "Well, thank you very much, Mrs. Brand; sorry to have taken up so much of your time," and departed.

When Meg finished work, he was waiting for her in the parking lot, leaning against her car, smoking. "Nice car," he said. "Going to miss it?"

"Shall I leave it in the Brand garage?"

"Of course, with a tag on it, 'Happy Thanksgiving Nana.' That is," he added, "I assume you'd want to leave it."

"Of course."

"Lots of cars around: mine, such as it is; Dad's; Mom's. You'll want your own if, with Clara with us, you're willing to work awhile."

"I could scrape up the down payment on a compact."

"Good. May I tell Sarah you'll have dinner with us tomorrow night? This time I'll pick you up and bring you home. Don't chicken out."

"I won't."

He said, "And from tomorrow night on, you wear your ring. This I spy, hole in the corner business is for the birds."

"All right," she said.

"Around seven," he said. He opened the door for her, leaned in and kissed her.

"Charles . . ." she protested. There were people walking to and from the parking lot, people coming out of the hospital or going in.

He said, "So we'll give them something to talk about, openly. They've been doing it anyway, for weeks."

Cornelia had dinner guests again that night. The conversation was as general as dinner was good. Meg was not asked to play bridge with Dr. Foster, his wife, and her sister; they did not need her. She excused herself, stayed for a while with Clara, and then went to bed. The next morning while she was having her coffee she said to Morton, "Will you tell Mrs. Brand that I won't be here for dinner tonight?"

When she got back that afternoon, she did not go out to the tea table, but from the cars parked outside, the voices and clatter of china and silver, she presumed that it was Cornelia's day to entertain the Women's Guild.

Looking in on Clara she asked, "The Guild?" and Clara nodded. "I've already had Andrew down, scrubbed to the bone, to shake hands and be cooed at. . . . You going out?"

"To the Scotts." She got down on her knees beside Clara's chair, to Andrew's astonishment, and hugged her.

"Me too," said Andrew, and Meg obliged.

She did not go downstairs after Cornelia's guests left and was dressing when Cornelia rapped on her door. She came in, looked around the quiet room, picked up a book, laid it down again; and then took Andy's picture in her hands. She said, "I never liked this one."

"I like it best of all," Meg said.

Cornelia replaced the photograph. She said, "Morton tells me you're going out to dinner. With Charles?"

"To the Scotts," said Meg. "Charles will pick me up and bring me back. I won't be late."

Cornelia said, "You can stay all night, as far as I'm concerned," and walked out.

Andrew was asleep, and Cornelia and Clara were at dinner when Charles drove up. Meg went out to meet him, and he said, "Not so fast—mustn't forget our manners." He took her by the arm and walked her through the living room and into the dining room. He said, "Good evening, Aunt Cornelia and Clara. Where's Andrew?"

"Asleep," said Clara.

"I brought him something." He produced a package and said to Clara, "Better check it before you give it to him, for dangerous materials. I don't know when I last bought toys."

Clara opened the box. Cornelia after her "Good evening, Charles," was stonily silent.

It was a brown-yellow dog, clean, engaging, and with superb whiskers.

Charles explained. "That bunny of his is probably lethal by now. This thing takes to soap and water, or so they told me at the coffee shop. Besides it looks like Tiger." He turned to Cornelia. "That's our new puppy," he explained, "the one Andrew fell in love with at the house. The feeling was mutual."

Clara said, "I'm afraid he can't be easily weaned away from Bunny."

184

"Try him; he'll adjust; you'd be surprised how one nail drives out another. . . . Come along, darling, before Sarah burns the soup."

Only Clara spoke from the table to say, "Good night," as they left.

At the Scotts the mixed-breed puppy greeted them with initial enthusiasm and then went forlornly away. Charles said, "He thought we'd bring Andrew back with us," and, in the house Helen Scott said, "Once you're settled in Charles's little place—you'll love it, Meg, but it does need redecoration —I'll give Tiger to Andrew."

"And good riddance," said her husband. "I almost break my neck falling over him daily." He called the puppy to him and said, "He's a good pup—smart too—but he still makes mistakes. Hey . . ." But Charles had seized the dog and was rushing him outdoors.

"Charles," his father remarked comfortably, "is good in an emergency. I don't advise you to redecorate, Meg, until you've corrected such little lapses."

Meg said, "It would be wonderful for Andrew to have a dog; he loves them; he's never shown the slightest fear, but you mustn't give him yours."

"We can spare one," said Bill Scott. "We have his mother."

After dinner Charles announced, "I want to make this official." He took the jeweler's box from his pocket, put the ring on Meg's finger and kissed her. "Witnesses, too," he said. "Now, plans."

His mother said, "Until you know what Cornelia plans, you'd better wait. You said Meg wants a small wedding in church. Have you discussed it with Cornelia, Meg?"

"No," she said, flushing.

"You'd better," Helen said serenely. "You see you have her backed into a corner. She won't want to give you a wedding or come to whatever wedding you have—which we'd like to give you, incidentally. On the other hand—because she feels deeply about her position in Melton and because any rumor or gossip relating to her would upset her—I don't see how she can get out of being present."

"She could take another cruise," said Meg and then desolately, "I don't want a reception. I just want to go to church and be married. She won't talk about it to me, Helen."

"I think she'll change her mind," said Helen. Her husband and son looked at her sharply and Bill Scott said uneasily, "What makes you say that?"

Helen smiled. She said, "Sooner or later you have to talk about things. I'm going upstairs now, and taking Meg with me. She'll be back presently, Charles."

They went up to the big pleasant bedroom where Helen waved Meg to a chair, and cast herself on the double bed with pillows behind her head. She said, "Don't get the notion that I'm an invalid. I'm not. But I don't sleep well and I tire easily. . . . You've never seen Charles's sister's picture, have you? Over there on the dresser, with the children's pictures." Sturdy youngsters and an attractive young woman, looking like her mother.

"The twins," said Helen, "are adorable." She studied Meg. "Will you tell me what troubles you, aside from the knowledge that Cornelia Brand and the Scotts haven't been friends in years?"

"Charles didn't?"

"No."

Meg told her about Keith Lansing, and Helen laughed. She said, "How very like Cornelia to employ private investigators."

Meg said, "It all seems so foolish when I put it into words, but what troubles me most I can't even phrase . . . her attitude, the way she avoids being alone with me; and the foolish threats she tosses at me like—like little darts."

Helen said, "I'm going to ask you something. I'd like an honest answer. Did she tell you about me and Drew?"

"Drew?"

"Andy's father; we always called him that."

After a moment Meg said unhappily, "Yes."

"I thought so. Did you tell Charles she had?"

"No . . . I couldn't."

Helen said, "It was long ago, faraway, and not entirely as I fancy she told it to you. Drew's been dead for years. She can't hurt him any more. She could never hurt me. I had Bill, and, of course, Charles. Andy too, for that matter. That's another thing she hasn't forgiven me for; Andy was fond of us all. When he'd come here, after he was grown up, he called it an escape. I had an escape too, as, of course, you know. I haven't needed it for a long time, Meg. Please believe that."

"I do believe it," Meg said unsteadily.

Helen said, "Come here"; and made room for Meg to sit on the edge of the bed. She said dreamily, "My mother used to scream if people sat on the edges of beds; bad for mattresses." She put up her hand and brushed Meg's hair back. She said, "Such pretty hair . . . Charles is lucky, Meg—he's found you. I was beginning to think he'd never find anyone."

Meg asked smiling, "What about—what's her name—Martin."

"Oh, so you know that, too. That was just a sighing over the moon." She sat up and kissed the younger woman. She said, "I think in a very short time you'll have a satisfactory conversation with Cornelia. . . . Now let's talk clothes, and England. Charles says that Clara is willing to go with you, and sometime this coming week, I'll take you to see Charles's little house."

When Meg returned to the men, Charles and his father rose with their evening drinks in their hands and Charles

187

said, indicating a table and the tray, "I fixed you a short, light snort to celebrate the wearing of your ring."

She looked down at her hand, and smiled. "It's beautiful," she said.

"Sit down," suggested her host, "and let's drink to the future. . . . Was Helen all right when you left her?"

"Fine. She was going to read and listen to music."

He said, as if Meg had been an old friend or for years a member of the family, "She wears herself out emotionally; takes everything to heart. Seems as if she's trying to make up for the years when she didn't." He looked at the glass in his hand. He said, "No reason why we shouldn't have a respectable libation before dinner; nowadays she says so often enough. But when she was battling with her . . . illness, Charles and I fell into this habit. And unless we're going out, she goes upstairs early—not to sleep," he added.

"Well," said Charles, "cheers." He regarded Meg over his glass. "Lots of things to iron out yet, don't let it upset you."

Taking her home, he asked, "What did you and Mom talk about?"

"Oh, clothes and such; and she's taking me to see your house next week."

"She's right. It needs redecorating. All in good time. Did she talk about Cornelia?"

"She just said she thought I'd have a satisfactory conversation with her soon."

"Did she say what makes her think so?" He added, "I can't imagine anyone having a satisfactory conversation with the sphinx."

"No, she didn't explain. It sounded rather like a prediction."

"Maybe it was."

She was beginning to be perceptive about his moods; she couldn't see his face clearly, but his tone was somber.

"It bothers you?" she asked.

"Yes. Wait until you really get to know my mother. She's gentle and quiet; she wasn't always, as Dad intimated. She used to be—well—lively, unpredictable, and she's always been stubborn. You must be attracted to stubborn people; Andy, for one; me, my parents, and of course Cornelia. Maybe attraction's the wrong word there."

Meg said, laughing, "I'm not easily swayed myself."

Charles wasn't listening. He said, "I hope to God it doesn't come to that."

"To what?" she asked, bewildered.

"The ace up my sleeve. I'd hoped not to use it, but I'm afraid my mother will."

Fifteen

AFTER A WHILE Meg said, "I don't understand you, darling," and he answered obscurely, "I hope you never will." The car shot into the Brand driveway. He said, "I'm not thinking of us, only of my mother."

He thought: She'd do anything, anything to make things smooth and easy for me and Meg, even if it threw her back into that . . . wretchedness. But I can't say anything, no one can say anything—if she meant what I think she did, talking to Meg.

They said good night in their customary fashion and Meg went into the house, performed the ritual of locks and lights, and went upstairs. Clara opened her door. She said, "You're early."

"I haven't the slightest idea what time it is." Meg held out her left hand under the hall lights. "Look," she said.

Clara drew her into the room, took her hand and looked as bidden. She said, "It's lovely."

"He gave it to me that night at Bassett's, but I asked him to keep it until things were straightened out."

"And are they?"

"No. But tonight, he insisted I wear it."

"He's right. High time."

"How's Andrew?"

"Sleeping of course."

"With old Bunny or new Tiger?"

Clara's face darkened. She said, "He doesn't have the toy Charles brought him. After you'd left his grandmother took it from me. She said she'd buy him something else."

"*Something else?* Where's the stuffed dog?"

"In the trash, outside. She went into her office with it, then she came back and walked through the kitchen. I saw it in her hands; later, I checked. She took scissors to it I expect."

For a moment they regarded each other in silence. And then Clara said, "Charles bought it at the coffee shop gift counter in the hospital. There'll be others there if she intends to duplicate it, Meg."

After a while Meg said, "I think this scares me more than anything else." She thought: The blind, destructive hatred . . .

Clara said carefully and low, though the door was closed. "She—she does tear things up if they don't suit her. . . . Haven't you noticed?"

"No—well—yes. Recently I've seen her twisting hand-kerchiefs, until they tore. I thought she was just nervous. She keeps everything suppressed, Clara; she has ever since I've known her."

"And long before that," Clara said. "I haven't dared speak to Dr. Foster about it—not that I often see him alone—but if I did, he'd say something to her."

"Well," said Meg as lightly as she could, "that's one way of getting rid of repressions, tearing things up, smashing them."

"Does that include people?" asked Clara.

After a moment Meg said, "Sometimes."

"Not you," Clara said sharply. "You've plenty of spirit. Andy never had any use for girls that hadn't."

"Heaven knows I haven't shown much spirit, as you call it, since I came here."

"No one expected you to; look at the way you came. I

won't forget the first time I saw you, or the months before Andrew was born; you were healthy enough," said Clara dispassionately, "but spineless. You just did what the doctor and Mrs. Brand told you. Half the time you didn't see what was around you. By the time you began to see, it was almost too late."

"Andrew . . ." said Meg slowly.

"Andrew's a baby," said Clara; "no real harm's been done."

"This whole miserable situation revolves around him, Clara. And baby or not, she's managed to attach him to her."

"He'll forget," said Clara, and added, "He's attached to me, too. That ever worry you?"

"No. You love him, you provide security. But you don't try to possess him."

"Nor his father either," said Clara. "I won't say that I didn't want to—I was young then; I thought I'd never have a child."

"Why not?"

Clara said, "I wasn't what you'd call a beauty. And my mother depended on me. Oh, I had some offers, two widowers, one good-looking drunk who wanted me to reform him." She laughed shortly.

"You could have worked things out for your mother."

"Maybe. But I couldn't leave Andy. I guess I was trying to see that he grew up on his own. I needn't have worried. He and his mother—that was a battlefield from the time he was six or seven. It was his father he cared for."

"He said very little about him to me."

"He would have if he'd had time," said Clara. "It went pretty deep. He resented his mother's dominance. He said to me more than once, 'Why does he let her boss him around?' He was very young, but he saw a lot. And his father's death just about destroyed him. He was at the university when it happened. He said to me after the funeral that his father didn't want to live. He didn't think there was anything to live for.' "

Meg asked appalled. "He didn't *kill* himself?"

"No. He was in a way a believing man. It was a heart attack. Maybe he brought it on; he never took care of himself no matter what she said. He was like eaten up inside—and outside as if he'd been erased."

"Andy escaped."

"Andy was made of other stuff. He had a lot of his mother in him, only it shaped up differently. Andy didn't want to dominate anyone but himself. . . . Look, go to bed, you have to work tomorrow. I've got things pretty clear in my head. I'll tell Mrs. Brand in the next day or so. I have to go to the bank tomorrow; I've told her that. I get there now and then, it's nothing new. I'll take Andrew; Ramsay will drive us. . . . Now, go to bed for heaven's sake."

Meg went to bed. She set her alarm and lay in darkness, her arms behind her head. For a little while she thought of Charles, then of Helen Scott, shifting back to Charles again and what he had said, inexplicably, of his mother. But before she slept she thought most about the glimpse Clara had given her of Andy's father, of Andy.

She thought of human relationships. Books explained them, philosophers, psychiatrists, psychologists, and the clergy. Books were written in simple terms for the layman; and a large percentage of them had become amateur analysts. Yet there'd always been an X factor which no one had fathomed—the something which didn't solve out; most of the body's secrets had been explored, if not all, and it was believed, the mind's. Yet there was something beyond these, also beyond genes, environments, influences, and traumatic experiences.

Science could split the atom. Science could pigeonhole the personality, split or not. But there was still a stretch of country science had not yet traveled, uncharted, undefined, and mysterious.

On the next day Meg was working and after an early

lunch and Andrew's nap, Clara dressed him and herself to go to the bank.

Cornelia was in her office when Clara and Andrew presented themselves. Cornelia said, "I'm not too busy, Clara, I could take him for you. I don't expect anyone later."

"I promised him the drive."

"Drive," repeated Andrew, looking stormy.

"I told him he could sit with Ramsay."

Andrew gave his grandmother his heart-melting smile and Cornelia said, "Well, in that case . . . Actually I do have some desk work to do and as long as you're going to the bank, will you cash a check for me; and stop at Hopkins' and at Greer's?"

Hopkins' was her jeweler; Greer's a toy shop. She pulled a note pad toward her, and said, "I'd like Andrew to have a . . ." She shook her head as he looked up alertly, and spelled aloud "T–O–Y."

Clara gave Andrew a slight push. "Run and see if Ramsay's there," she suggested, and he trotted off obediently.

"Another Bunny?" said Cornelia. "And there's a package they're holding for me at Hopkins'."

Ramsay came; Andrew and Clara departed. The Mortons were presumably in the kitchen. Cornelia was making notes— The Queen was in her counting house—relevant to changes in her last will and testament. She had talked them over with Amos Perry, who hadn't approved, but he was in no position to say so, merely to recommend that she think it over, write it out, and then make an appointment to see him again.

A car came up the driveway, stopped in front of the house, and Helen Scott got out.

She stood there by the car, touching the door. She noticed that her hand shook slightly. No one heard or saw her, a tall, too slender woman in a rose-colored dress, hatless, gloveless, carrying only a big straw handbag.

She looked for several minutes at the house, remembering

the last time she had seen it, the last time she had entered the front door, the last time it had closed behind her. How long had it been? Fifteen, sixteen years . . . a century?

She touched the bell, and heard it chime. Waiting, half turning away, she thought: There's still time to get in the car and drive off.

Morton, pulling on his jacket, hurried from the kitchen. Cornelia thought impatiently: Who can that be? She had been immersed in the problems of her grave responsibility, writing down her wishes on the big pad. If Andrew were still a minor when she died, the money, in trust, would be managed by the bank and the Perry office. His mother would have no part in the administration of the funds, although she was, as Amos had pointed out, Andrew's natural guardian. Andrew would have an allowance, at home, and in school; he would come into some of the income when he was eighteen. At twenty-one, much more. The principal, at twenty-five? She thought also about the house; it would be his, then, and the trust would keep it up; Clara, if she outlived Cornelia, would look after him as long as he needed her.

There were so many things to consider.

Someone knocked, and she said, abstracted, "Yes?" and Morton came in. She saw that he was agitated.

"Well, Morton, what is it?" she asked. She'd forgotten the chimes, ringing.

He stammered a little. "Mrs. Sc-Scott to s-see you, Mrs. Brand."

When he had opened the hall door, he had not immediately identified the caller; she had altered. But she'd known him, and called him by name.

Cornelia experienced a numbing shock, and then blinding anger. She said harshly, "Tell Mrs. Scott I'm not . . . no, wait a moment." Not before servants, Cornelia; never permit them to see you disconcerted, or out of control.

She pushed the paper and pencils aside, picked up her

handkerchief and said evenly, "Very well. Show her in . . ."
She hesitated, twisting the scrap of linen. Not the living
room; when last she'd seen Helen Scott, except from a distance, it had been in the living room. To her horror she
found herself wondering how often it had been repainted
since.

"Show her in here please, Morton," she said.

Morton went back to the hall where Helen waited and
said, "If you'll come with me, please, Mrs. Scott."

He'd always liked her; been sorry for her, poor thing; not
so Mrs. Morton. He'd thought, at the time: Women are
usually harder on women than men were.

She asked him now about his wife, as they walked to the
study, and he answered, "She's fine, Mrs. Scott."

"Tell her I asked for her, will you?"

He had left the office door open, and Cornelia rose and
said, "How are you, Helen?" and then to Morton, she said,
"That will be all for now, Morton. Please close the door."

Helen looked around the room. The last time she'd been
in it, it hadn't been Cornelia's office but her husband's study,
which Cornelia often usurped. He'd said once to Helen, half
laughing, half serious, "A man has no privacy, none at all."

"Sit down," said Cornelia carelessly. "You've lost a good
deal of weight, Helen."

"I suppose I have. You look very well."

"I am. I take care of myself."

Meaningless the words; the silence which followed heavy.
And then Cornelia asked, "Why did you come to see me?
Is it about Meg and Charles?"

"Yes."

Cornelia picked up a pencil. Sunlight came in and was
a little unkind to her. She said, "You disapprove of this—
this alliance, as I do?"

Helen said, letting the sun search out her own lines of
fatigue and indecision, welcoming the light warmth on her
face and hair, "On the contrary, Cornelia."

"Oh! Then what have we to discuss?"

Helen thought: I can look at her and not feel humiliated; I can look at her and not feel sick.

She said, almost gaily, "Nothing really. I came to tell you that you must stop interfering."

Cornelia flushed deeply. "Interfering?" she repeated. "What earthly right have you to march into my house and tell me what or what not to do?"

Helen said, "You could make things a little easier for them, Cornelia."

Cornelia laughed. She said, "Such as give my son's widow a wedding and hold a reception here?"

"I don't think she'd want that," said Helen, "but I'm sure it would be wise for you to attend the ceremony." She added, "You know, of course, that Bill is greatly loved in Melton; not even your most subtle or most direct methods have been able to affect his standing in the town and at the hospital. Charles is also loved and has been since he was a child. There would be a good deal of talk, and not in your favor if you failed to make an appearance . . . with, of course, little Andrew."

Cornelia said, "Nonsense. I intend to go away at the time, taking Andrew and, of course, Clara with me."

Helen said, "But Andrew is going to England."

"I will not permit him to be taken out of this country."

"You have no choice. Meg is his mother."

"He will stay here with me and Clara," said Cornelia.

"But Clara's going to England with them," Helen said.

Cornelia looked at her with utter disbelief. She said, "The last time you were in this house you were staggering drunk. Now the obvious conclusion is that you're out of your mind."

"Oh, the last time," said Helen. "Yes, I was drunk, and not, I might add, for the last time, though it's been a long while now since that final occasion."

"Exactly what did you mean about Clara?"

"Just what I said. She'll tell you herself. Cornelia, tell me just one thing. Did you believe what Drew must have told you when he came home that night?"

"Morning. No I didn't believe him," said Cornelia, "and I wouldn't believe anything you tell me now."

Helen said, "If he told you the truth, he said that when he got me back to my house I had passed out. He carried me in and upstairs, he roused Sarah, who undressed me. Drew waited outside; he also called Dr. Kimberly and waited until he came, and then until Bill got home, which was toward morning. Sarah has always been able to verify this."

"Sarah would lie her head off for you."

"Of course."

"And Kimberly's been dead for years."

"But I'm not," said Helen, "nor Bill nor Charles. . . ." She picked up the handbag beside her. "I never expected to do this, Cornelia. Let me tell you something about myself. No, don't ring for Morton. Poor old man, why embarrass him? I don't intend to leave now. Do you know why I drank? Because I was a selfish, spoiled young woman; because I knew that Bill's profession came first with him, before me; and because I was lonely and demanding. Bill grew to understand that. I may have you to thank for his understanding," she said thoughtfully. "When you came to see him, you told him what you believed—or merely said— was the truth. He knew it wasn't. He threw you out; he wouldn't let you see me."

Cornelia said, "I didn't wish to see any of you ever again."

Helen said, "Drew was unfaithful to you, Cornelia; not with me, not that night . . . but in his mind; and probably had been and went on being unfaithful, not merely in his mind." She opened the handbag and took a number of letters from it, held together by an elastic band.

She said, "Do you want to read these? You recognize Drew's handwriting? They are letters he wrote me after that night, asking me to meet him, asking if he could come to

198

the house whenever Bill happened to be away; yet excoriating himself for asking, as Bill was his close friend. . . . There's even one asking if I'd go away with him . . . he drank too," she said steadily. "He wouldn't have had the courage to leave you, and he couldn't leave Andy. But here they are, read them for yourself."

"No."

Helen said, "He was a very unhappy man. He wasn't in love with me, Cornelia, nor with any of the women who may have met him on the trips he sometimes took. I think he was in love with you, once, before you were married."

Cornelia said, "I don't believe this."

"Read the letters."

She put out a hand, took one, read a few lines, tossed it back. "I did everything for him," she said.

"Everything? Money, Cornelia, lots of money. Nothing else; no warmth, no love, no compassion."

Helen Scott had known Cornelia since girlhood. She had never seen her cry, not at her parents' funerals, not at anything. She was crying now, slow, painful tears; her face was ugly with the shock of what she was inwardly seeing. "I loved him."

"You've never loved anyone in your life," said Helen; "not Drew, except as a belonging; not Andy, except as an extension of yourself which he wasn't, and now the baby."

Cornelia was not listening. She asked, putting the ripped handkerchief to her eyes and cheeks, "Has anyone else seen these?"

"Bill, of course; and Charles, when he was old enough to hear things and to wonder."

"Charles!" It was an exclamation of despair. Then she asked, "Andy?"

"Drew was his father," said Helen, "nothing on earth would have made me show these to Andy; and if you're wondering if Charles told him, he didn't. How could he?"

Helen rose and touched Cornelia on the shoulder. But Cornelia shuddered away from her. Helen said, "I'm sorry I had to do this to you, but my son is very important to me; and Meg's beginning to be. Still I'm sorry." She picked up the letters and put them in her handbag and Cornelia demanded. "Give them to me."

"No, It isn't time to destroy them, yet."

"You intend to show them to Meg?" Cornelia asked slowly.

"Only if it's necessary. I hope it won't be. In a day or so, perhaps you'll talk to her, and tell her—I started to say tell her that everything's all right, but it isn't and won't be. You could say, though, that you'll be at her wedding, even if you really don't intend to be."

She went out. Morton, not having been summoned, was not in the hall. She felt unsteady. She thought: Drew told her the truth of course and whether or not she believed him, she told him she didn't. He had that to live with the rest of his life just as I've had to live with the other side of the coin. Bill's believing the truth when he heard it, from Drew first, then me. Just as I've had to live with my own weakness and stupidity.

She got in the car and started it. She thought for the first time in years: I could use a drink. She shook her head; she couldn't use one, not ever again; and driving away from the Brand house she thought: And what's more, I *don't* need it.

Sixteen

C ORNELIA listened to the car drive away. Then she got
up, and left her office. She held fast to the stair rail
and moved slowly and carefully, as if she had aged
twenty years. She went into her room, took a tranquilizer,
and lay down. She remembered she had left the notes concerning her will on her office desk. She would have to put
them away before anyone came. She went back painfully to
get them and locked them in her bureau drawer. Tomorrow
she would write Amos Perry and mail him what she'd
written to be drawn up in proper form and signed. She
thought: I'm not equal to seeing him now.

As she felt the shock of Helen's visit and resultant panic
receding, she began to think more clearly. There are times
when the truth or part of it is indicated. She couldn't call
Morton and instruct him that he was not to say she'd had an
unexpected visitor. Perhaps he wouldn't anyway, but he
might. She supposed he'd been talking about it to his wife.
What went on in an employer's household was the domes-
tics' drama. She thought of Clara; she thought: That's not
true. After all these years it can't be. I won't say anything.
If it's true, she'll tell me. She began to marshal her arguments.
You don't come right out and say, "After all I've done for
you . . ." Clara didn't have to be told what Cornelia had
done for her.

She thought: If I try to sleep for a little, I can manage
dinner.

As if nothing had happened.

Clara returned from her errands. She had the jeweler's package with her, the money for Cornelia (in a neat envelope), and for Andrew the new bunny. But more or less disdaining it, he carried it casually by the ears.

"You must thank Nana."

"Old bunny," said Andrew with outthrust lower lip.

"He's still here; he and the new bunny could get to be good friends."

Morton came into the hall. He said, "Mrs. Brand rang before you came in; she's going to take a nap. She'll see you at dinner."

He went back to the kitchen and reported to his wife that Clara seemed sort of nervous and he couldn't remember when Mrs. Brand had taken a nap. "She didn't even want tea," he added in astonishment.

And Mrs. Morton said, "Didn't think I'd live to see the day that Mrs. Scott came to this house. No wonder She was upset."

"She" with a capital S, was always Cornelia.

Meg came home to find everything quiet. No one in the sun porch, no cars parked outside. She went upstairs to the nursery. The new bunny sat forlornly in a corner, and Andrew was preoccupied with his little train, the elder bunny clutched in his arm.

"New addition to the family?" asked Meg.

"Mrs. Brand had me buy it at Greer's, when Andrew and I went out today."

"Did he select it?"

"No. She did, by remote control."

Meg picked up the stuffed animal. She asked her son, "What's his name?"

Andrew shook his head. He went to his mother, took the toy from her hand and threw it back in the corner.

Clara said, "That isn't kind, Andrew," and Meg said, "I'm surprised at you. Poor bunny."

Andrew shook his head again.

"Maybe," said Meg, sighing, "the dog would have received the same treatment."

"I don't think so," Clara told her. "The dog was something else; not a replacement."

"Has he thanked his grandmother?"

"Not yet, she's taking a nap; she'll see us at dinner—but not Andrew; she told Morton that Andrew would eat in the nursery."

"Headache again?" asked Meg with her worried little scowl—a replica of her son's as she would have seen had she been looking at him.

"I don't know. I've picked up the alligator traveling clock at Hopkins', cashed a check for her, and bought the bunny. I haven't seen her. I found your mail in the hall, and put it in your room. Mrs. Brand's is still there; she told Morton she'd see it later."

Meg's mail: two more postals from Portugal, one giving the date when the Wilsons would be home, and a letter from Keith Lansing. She opened it in her room with misgivings. He inquired how she and Andrew were; he said, Francesca had been delivered of a boy, which pleased them all very much. And added, "I had a curious letter from Mrs. Brand. I haven't replied to it yet. She asked if I could come to Melton because she'd like to talk with me. I can't imagine what about. Will you tell her I'll answer shortly, but that I can't come, much as I'd like to. As soon as Francesca's able, we'll be going off on a cruise, leaving the kids, including Keith, Jr., with the nurse and the Wainwrights. Maybe I'll bring Fran to see you before snow flies—she's anxious to meet you and to see Scotty again."

So much for the pending divorce and the Wainwrights' rejection of their son-in-law's project. Meg thought: Keith always liked to complain in a half serious, wholly exaggerated way. She remembered when he'd come to the apartment. You'd think, if you believed him, that the hospital was falling apart and only Dr. Lansing held it together with courage, patience, and fast thinking. It was wholly possible that he'd complained to Cornelia. She could almost hear him doing so: "Not that I'm not happy in my work, Mrs. Brand, and the hospital plans mean a great deal to me." At this point he'd probably said, "I wish Fran were more involved. She's always fearful during pregnancies, she and her mother." He'd probably shrugged and said smiling, "When my son—or maybe sons—grow up, I'll advise them never to marry a run-home-to-mother-girl."

Well, something like that anyway, and out of this meager material, manufactured simply to hold the interest of his hostess and arouse her sympathy, Cornelia had woven a fantasy, a plot, and a plan.

COCKTAILS AS USUAL; the martinis and sherry in the living room. Cornelia had seen Andrew briefly and he'd had to be prompted by Clara to say, "Thank you, Nana." She'd cast one look at the recent acquisition in the corner and said quite cheerfully, "I thought he'd like it." Clara had predicted carefully, "All in good time," and Cornelia had then admitted, with her purposeful candor, "You'll think me silly, I daresay, but I threw out the toy Charles bought."

"I know; I saw it in the trash."

Cornelia then said, "Frankly I didn't want Andrew to have it, for a variety of reasons."

At dinner Meg spoke of Keith's letter. She reported the new baby; and the plans. "He said you'd written him, Nana, and that he'd answer presently."

Cornelia said, "How nice about the new baby. . . . Yes I wrote. I thought if he were anywhere near or wanted to make a special trip, I might be able to help him. I have the blueprints of our hospital and other material which I thought might give him some ideas." She then went on brightly, "I had a most unexpected visitor this afternoon, Meg, Charles's mother. I'm sorry you were at work."

Clara put down her fork and picked up her water glass. Meg sat quiet, without words.

"She's changed markedly," said Cornelia, "much too thin."

Meg asked, "But why did she call?"

"Oh . . . naturally because of your engagement." Her glance touched on Meg's left hand. She said, "I see you're wearing a ring—it's very handsome—and that, I suppose, makes it official. Of course your aunt should properly make the announcement, but at the distance, and with the wedding date not far off, perhaps you'd wish me to?"

Meg said, "If you like, Nana."

She was stunned. The graceful acceptance of defeat was simply not in Cornelia's nature. "It isn't a question of liking." Cornelia lifted her bright brown eyes to Meg and said smiling, "You seem to have charmed Helen which is, of course, very satisfactory. She didn't tell me if the exact date has been settled upon."

"It hasn't been," said Meg.

"Well, settle it then; there's so much to do. You prefer a church wedding, I hope?"

Meg nodded and Cornelia said, "I suggest a small reception here. . . . Have you told your aunt?"

"Not the date, or all of our plans." She hesitated. "I thought I'd call her, she'll be home from Portugal soon."

"I'd like to speak with her too," Cornelia said, cordially. "I wish she and her husband could be here; he could give you away." She did not add "again," but the word was there, heavy, if unspoken, between them.

Meg said, "But we'll be seeing them in England."

"That's right. You should have a most pleasant reunion and wedding trip. Andrew will miss you."

"Andrew," said Meg, white, "is going with us."

"Oh? I'd hoped you had reconsidered. After all, a small child on a wedding trip . . . I imagine you won't stay all the time with your aunt. I'm afraid Andrew will be very unhappy with strangers."

Clara opened her mouth to speak and Meg looked at her in warning. Cornelia saw the look, and the warning. So that was it! Helen had been telling the truth.

She pushed aside her dessert. She said, "If you'll excuse me, I think I'll go to my room; it's been a rather too exciting day. Not," she added rising, "that it wasn't amiable of Helen to appear with the olive branch; I doubt I would have had the—courage. But then her situation is different from mine."

She went steadily from the room and Morton came in and asked, "Will Mrs. Brand take coffee?"

"She didn't say so; she's just gone upstairs."

He brought the coffee to the living room, vanished, and Clara said, "I was going to tell her," and Meg said, "I know, but I think perhaps she's had enough for the time being."

Clara said vigorously, "It's time this was all cleared up, Meg. What changed her mind, for pity's sake?"

"Charles's mother," said Meg, "and I have no idea how." She thought: I wonder if she told Charles or his father when she reached home?

Helen had not. Her husband was waiting for her when she drove in, coming out to the car, saying crossly, "Where in hell have you been?"

Exactly there Helen thought. She said, "Oh, just around. It's a nice day; I had some errands to do."

"Well, spending your old man's money doesn't seem to have done you any harm."

"On the contrary," said his wife, "it's done me good."

She felt light and gay and well. The puppy ran around the front of the house and up the steps and fell upon her with love. She said, stopping to scratch behind his ears, "Andrew will love him."

"His mother won't like the idea of separation."

The mother, who had clearly married beneath her, came to join the group and Helen said, "She'll get used to it, as most mothers must; besides they won't be far away."

Charles came home in time for dinner. He said, during it, "I have to go back to the hospital." He yawned and added that he'd like to sleep for a week. "But I'll phone Meg from here. I saw her twice today—somehow when she floats around the corridors, it's as if she were on another planet. But," he added happily, "I don't think it was all work. She's wearing her ring and there will be a lot of people drifting by to felicitate her."

"Her?" said his mother. "What about you?"

"I no longer rate," he said. "Think of all the broken hearts strewing the immaculate floors. One more eligible crossed off the list. Meg will be the one. The girls would like to snatch her baldheaded, but they'll restrain themselves."

His father remarked that modesty was Charles's chief characteristic.

He stayed with them for a short while after dinner, then rose to make his telephone call, but the bell rang before he reached the instrument. Sarah took it in the kitchen and came hurrying out. She said, "It's Mrs. Brand, Charles; she's awful upset."

Charles picked up the telephone in the living room. He said, "What's up?" listened, said, "I'll meet you there," and hung up.

"Is anything wrong?" asked Helen instantly.

"Cornelia. She's had a seizure of some sort. Foster's on his way and the ambulance. I'll be in touch," and was gone, hatless, coatless, and running.

Helen leaned back against her chair. She was ashen and her husband went over and took her hand. He called Sarah, hovering in the hall. "Water," he said, "and the tablets; there are some downstairs."

Sedatives which Helen occasionally took. He said, "Don't try to speak, sweetheart." He half carried her to the couch and put her down. Sarah brought the water and tablets and Scott said, "Swallow these and lie still."

When her color began to return, she said, in an odd pinched voice, "I wasn't going to faint."

"Had you been, I wouldn't have given you what I did."

"I"—she put her hands over her face—"I feel so guilty."

"You went to see Cornelia?" he asked quietly.

"Yes."

"Why?"

After a moment she said, "Two can play at blackmail."

Scott reddened. He said, "You took Drew's letters with you?"

"Yes, Bill."

He said heavily, "But they posed no threat, Helen. They didn't contain any information you'd ever propose to publish. Cornelia must have known what was in them."

"How do we know? How do we know what Drew told her?"

"He told her the truth."

"We'll never know," she said, "if he told her the truth and she preferred to twist it into a lie; we'll never know, if he told her, whether she believed him or not, or whether she deliberately——"

"Oh, hush," Scott broke in. "I thought you'd destroyed them long ago."

"She asked who'd seen them. I said you and Charles. She wanted me to give them to her to destroy. I said, not yet. She asked if I planned to show them to Meg, and I said, if necessary, though I didn't intend to." After a moment she said wearily, "I don't know that I did it as much for Charles and Meg as for myself; for the satisfaction of making her look at herself."

"You're going upstairs now," he told her. "I'm putting you to bed."

"You won't leave me?"

"Of course not. And Charles will call us or come home soon. Please don't cry, darling."

208

Charles was at the hospital when the ambulance and Dr. Foster came. Arrangements had already been made—a private room, nurses around the clock, one of whom Cornelia had had before and liked, a Miss Barlow.

He found Meg in the waiting room. She was drawn and white. He said, sitting down, "I haven't talked to Foster yet. I shall. What did he say to you?"

"Cerebral accident," said Meg, scarcely moving her lips. "She's not conscious."

Charles said, "It may not be a bad one, Meg. And it was in the cards."

She opened her eyes wide. "What do you mean?"

"She's had one before."

"When?"

"After she got back from her cruise. . . ."

"But she didn't tell Andy!"

"No, and no one else was allowed to either. Meg, stop shaking."

"So much of it," she said, "is my fault; and Clara's sitting home wondering how much was hers."

"Why?"

"Before we'd finished dinner Nana—Cornelia—went upstairs. Later, Clara went in to talk to her. She said she had to get it over. Oh, Charles, she'd saved and saved from her salary; and she figured the sale of the house would more than make up the rest of what Cornelia had spent on the nursing home. She even talked to Dr. Foster—he's part of Cornelia's gift to Clara—who said that, despite her age, Clara's mother could live six months, even a year—her heart is very strong— and that it would be safe for Clara to leave her for a while. Of course she didn't tell him with whom."

"Then what happened?"

"I don't know exactly. I stayed downstairs. I thought you'd phone. Clara wasn't in with her long. When I heard her go back into her room, I went up. She told me Cornelia took it pretty well. Clara showed her the bank books and all Cornelia said was, 'Don't be stupid.' Then Clara came away. As Clara left Cornelia was taking some papers from the bureau; she had a pencil and a pen."

Both Meg and Clara heard the crash and ran to the room. Clara got there first, but the door was locked. Clara ran downstairs for Morton who had duplicate keys and he and Mrs. Morton came pounding up. The old man's unsteady hands managed the key and they all went in.

Meg said, "I blame myself, Clara blames herself." She looked at him levelly. "And your mother does by now," she added.

"My mother?"

"She came to see Cornelia this afternoon; I was working, Clara was out, getting her interest totted up."

"My God!" said Charles. He left her and went to a telephone booth and called his father.

"Is Mom all right?"

"Yes. How's Cornelia?"

"Cerebral accident. I haven't talked to Foster yet. I'm waiting to see him. Just tell Mom she'll be all right."

He went back to Meg. He said, "Well that tears it."

"But what could she possibly have said?"

He took her hands. There were others in the waiting room who watched the two curiously. "I don't know, Meg. All I can say is, she'd kept letters from Uncle Andrew," he told her softly. "My father saw them, and I did, too, much later. Andy's father wrote them to my mother. In them was the plain truth about what happened or didn't happen. Dad was very fond of Andrew Brand; so was my mother; and they both loved Andy. No problem would be solved by calling Cornelia a liar to her face, so my father did so, only once, on the day she came storming to the house to demand to see Mom and make her stupid accusations. That's when he threw her out."

"Did Andy know?"

"That they quarreled, yes; about the letters, no. What purpose would have been served? He always disliked his mother, Meg."

After a while Dr. Foster emerged, after the spinal tap and other tests. He said to Meg, "You can look in on her; Miss Barlow's there."

Meg went in and stood by the bed. This was an old woman, unconscious, as remote as the stars. The tears ran down Meg's face, and Miss Barlow said, "Isn't it dreadful? Such a wonderful woman. I was with her the last time, you know."

Meg remembered that Cornelia had helped Elsie Barlow through her training.

Charles motioned Dr. Foster into a small conference room. He asked, "How bad is it?"

"Well, we won't know for a while, but not too bad, I think. No worse than last time. I've warned her repeatedly," said Foster, sighing. "I did everything I could. But with a blood pressure like hers. . . . Was she upset about anything? I asked Meg and she said she didn't know."

"Nor do I," said Charles.

"Who knows anything about her?" asked his colleague. "Other people quarrel, scream, throw things; whatever affected her, she always repressed. The first time it was of course Andy's marriage, yet she kept the lid on that until after she came home from her trip. Oh, congratulations, by the way . . . and I'll be in touch."

When Meg came out, Charles drove her home. He said, firmly, "I'd better go see Clara with you."

So they went upstairs. Clara's light burned and she was walking up and down the room. She said, abruptly, "I picked up some papers from the floor. Mrs. Brand had evidently started to sign them."

Meg said, "We'll put them downstairs in her desk, Clara."

"How bad is it, Charles?"

"Foster says we won't know for a while. I don't think, very." He put his arm around Clara and she leaned against him gratefully. He said, "Stop blaming yourself . . . you too, Meg . . . and I hope I can persuade my mother not to." He thought: After all, in a way Cornelia's won; they'll all blame themselves . . . me too, in a way.

Meg said, "We'll have to alter our plans."

"Oh, no, we won't. If Cornelia recovers, as she did the last time, I don't say she'll dance at our wedding, but she could be there. If not, she has a legitimate excuse."

"Now I can't leave her," said Clara.

"You've already left," said Charles. "She'll want no part of you. I think Elsie Barlow will come home with her. She did last time. She has an unbounded admiration for Cornelia Brand."

"But what will we do now?" asked Meg wearily.

"You'll stay right here. You and Clara can cope with Cornelia's friends, the telephone, and mail. You'd better ask Mrs. Elgin for a leave of absence; in these circumstances she'll grant it. After all that, Elsie can manage; she's very efficient. I'll stop and speak to the Mortons on the way out. I hardly said anything to the poor old boy when we came in."

He kissed Clara. He said, "You're going to like it with us." He kissed Meg and said, "If you and Clara have any sense, you'll take a shot of something out of a bottle, but I don't suppose you will. I'll go on home and wrestle with my mother's conscience, while you two are wrestling with yours. Believe me," he said from the doorway, "this could have happened any time, following something as trivial as a tree falling outside or a Board Meeting. Try to believe that; it's true."

When he'd gone, Meg began, "If she dies——"

Clara, her good healthy color back again, said, "She won't die."

She thought: Not until she signs those papers whatever they are. Whatever happens, she'd rather haunt us while she's alive. She also thought: There'll be plenty to cope with when she's well again; the tug of war over Andrew . . . And then she told herself: But Meg will have Charles and his parents, so she and Andrew will be in a safe place.